I0681237

A DARK FICTION LITERARY ANTHOLOGY

Volume 5

Edited by
N. Apythia Morges

Dark Alley Press

INK STAINS ANTHOLOGY
Volume 5

ISBN 13: 978-1-946050-05-2
ISBN 10: 1946050059

Dark Alley Press
http://www.darkalleypress.com

An imprint of Vagabondage Press LLC
PO Box 3563
Apollo Beach, Florida 33572
http://www.vagabondagepress.com

First edition printed in the United States of America and the United Kingdom, July 2017

10 9 8 7 6 5 4 3 2 1

Front cover art by Jetrel. Cover designed by Maggie Ward.

INK STAINS

A DARK FICTION LITERARY ANTHOLOGY

TABLE OF CONTENTS

AGENTS OF THE SERAPHIM

Michael Picco

"Thy dead men shall live, together with my dead body shall they arise."

— *Isaiah 26:19*

My name is not "Zane."

That was what the newspapers called me: "Killer Zane." I was dubbed this after writing "God is gracious" on the walls of those whom I have released from this veil of tears. I wrote exactly what I was instructed to write, nothing more. A journalist out of Chicago deduced that that was what the name Zane meant: "*God is gracious.*" Or perhaps it was one of those clever fellows at the FBI who worked this out and let it slip to the press. There is no clever *corollarium nomen* there. This name, or my "Christian" name, is not important. Only the six-winged Seraphim call me by my true and righteous name.

It's my fault, you see — the destruction of the world before you. Not directly, of course...events such as these rarely have a direct causal relationship with the outcome. But, if you were to pull the thread, I am ultimately responsible for what has occurred. I am a butterfly at the heart of the storm. God's hand in the affairs of men is subtle. It's chaos theory through Divine perspective — well beyond our puny understanding of the workings of the world. Beyond our understanding of sin and, more importantly in my case, the sin of disobedience.

Late last year, I killed a man. This is not a confession nor was it my first mission, but it demonstrates why I must do the things I do. The Seraphim must not be denied. His name was Abdul Jehangeer. Why did I kill this man, you ask? Was Abdul Jehangeer destined to become the next Pol Pot? Was he a brutal and ruthless serial murderer (like Killer Zane, perhaps)? Was he a terrorist? No. Jehangeer was a decent man, by all accounts: hard working and loyal. He watched football on Sundays and drove his mediocre car to his mediocre job.

His seed, however, had to be denied.

In the years to come, his marriages would result in a sizable brood: three sons and one daughter. In time, his children would eventually become statesmen: senators and diplomats. The policies that Jehangeer's children would shape would come to stabilize much of the Sub-Saharan region of Africa. This would, in turn, cause prosperity to return to these regions and result in the population swelling well beyond the region's capacity to manage. Eventually, a war over resources would erupt, and a limited nuclear exchange would take place. Millions would die. The resulting radioactive clouds would travel with the prevailing winds into the Middle East, contaminating the Holy Land for hundreds of years — killing hundreds of thousands of the Faithful who lived there or who returned there to worship in the blighted centuries that followed. More wars would follow. The world would turn barren.

Working through me, the Seraphim deny the world this fate by denying this one man his breath. The cascade of dominoes is prevented by removing just a single piece. God is gracious: by killing one, He has saved uncounted thousands. Yes, God is gracious. And we are, all of us, God's madmen.

The bite…it's starting to burn now. The flesh around the wound has gone grayish green. But then, does *The Bible* not say "the dead will be raised imperishable, and we will be changed"? Changed indeed! Somehow, I don't think this is what the Good Book had in mind.

How could I possibly know these things about Abdul Jehangeer? I am, after all, no prophet. The Seraphim *chose* me. They disclose these things *only to me*. But they are not revealed to me in pillars of fire or showers of gold like they were for the prophets of old! No…I receive no such splendors. They come to me instead as my victims. The slaughtered lambs which, one after the other, take the last one's wretched place as my guide. They are the avatars of the Seraphim. It's their voices that are all the same; that's how I know it's the Seraphim and not…something else. They are not like those who paw and moan and gurgle just beyond my door.

There is no rest for those creatures.

The avatar's eyes still have light in them. His Holy Fire! Perhaps, these are my pillars of fire — my revelation made manifest! Ill prepared was I when the Seraphim first spoke to me as a child. My mind wasn't ready to receive them in their splendor or able to withstand the other-worldliness of their appearance. Back then, I heard their messages in the rustling of leaves in the trees, the roar of water in a waterfall, the rumble of thunder in a storm. Sometimes, I heard their voices in the rush of blood through my veins. Then, as now, they answer my questions and soothe my mind when all I see is blood. The Seraphim keep me free, while Satan and his minions close about me.

He has many minions. And the wicked never rest.

His servants find no end to their torment. Even the release of death is denied them. They have no light in their eyes. Just a dull, dry stare. It is through the Seraphim that I confound these demons — those that walk like men, but are not. The Seraphim grant me shelter and ease the pain behind my eyes, but alas, not the burning beneath my skin. The Seraphim grant me peace, but not serenity, it seems. There is no redemption for failure. I am merely a man — neither evil nor divine — only fallible and weak. Which, of course, is why I am here, writing to you in these last hours.

My first revelation came when I was 14. My heart was purer then, and the Seraphim's voice boomed like brass in my ears. My mother was still alive then, if you could call it "living." She, my sister, and I had moved to into subsidized housing on the lower East Side, following my father's abandonment and subsequent death. My mother was a good woman, but drugs and dependency had broken her spirit and robbed her of her better judgement. But, God is gracious, and brought into our lives a preacher of his Word. A "revivalist" he called himself. He traveled from town to town, preaching the Word — sometimes in front of rag-tag congregations, sometimes alone, on street corners, a peeling sandwich board draped across his narrow shoulders. He bellowed and spat the Word from his clapboard pulpit until his voice grew hoarse and raspy. He would drive out demons and speak in tongues that only he understood. His eyes burned with a fire, but, not like the avatar's eyes do. There was a different fire alight in his eyes. I was the youngest and often forced to attend these events, when my sister, Nan, was not around to watch me.

It was winter when it happened, almost exactly a year to the day that my father died. I was coming home from school, and I remember how the chill had wormed its way through my thin jacket and had burrowed into the very marrow of my bones. I ached and shivered as I walked through the empty afternoon streets, below the elevated train. It passed overhead, and in its rumble, I heard the Seraphim for the first time: "Be swift!" It said. I looked around, but there were no people on the streets. But, even then, I knew that no mortal man could have such a voice. Part rumble, part groan of the city around me, the voice boomed through the din, like a radio broadcast bursting through static. "Be swift!" It said again. "Go home. Make no sound."

The man was there — the preacher — though, he had not preached in months. That is, except to us. As the winter had come on, we became his congregation. His flock. His lambs. I had become accustomed to him and his erratic behavior by then, but my sister had become more and more withdrawn. My mother had responded in her usual way. When I arrived, I found her lying on the couch, the needle still dangling from her arm. There was a lot of something still pooled in the syringe, so what had killed her had done so quickly. Someone was upstairs. I heard crying.

The Seraphim told me to go to my mother and take the syringe from her arm. Her warm and inviting arms were now cool to the touch. The liquid inside the syringe was milky brown, like blood mixed with milk and quicksilver. The needle came out of her arm with a scratching sound that I will never forget — as if the wound had dried and I was pulling it out of cardboard instead of flesh. The wound didn't bleed. The Seraphim cooed softly to me: "Upstairs. Be swift. Be silent." The voice carried on the blood as it roared through my ears.

The floor was old and full of loose boards, but it did not betray me as I approached the bedroom my sister and I shared. I could hear the rasp of bedsprings mingled with the preacher man's labored breathing as I approached the door. He was there, with his back to the door, my sister pressed beneath him. He hadn't entirely removed his trousers, but it was obvious what was happening. My sister's eyes were open but were locked on the ceiling, as if she were looking at something else entirely…something far away. Tears stained her face. Her hands were balled into fists as she pushed vainly against the preacher's bony shoulders.

Neither of them heard me as I stepped inside and plunged the syringe into the preacher man's neck, just below and behind his right ear, emptying it completely.

The preacher man was dead before he hit the ground. I was not blamed for his death. Bad smack had been reported all over the neighborhood. To the police, it was just another overdose death in a community filled with junkies. No doubt, the Seraphim deflected blame, clouded judgement — freeing me — so I could serve Them.

My sister was too young to care for me. We were separated and placed in different foster homes. She was adopted some years later. Her new family eventually moved to the West Coast. As years have passed, I've heard less and less from her — time and distance taking its toll. Familial ties, already strained from too much trauma and tragedy, have frayed and weakened, finally perishing from neglect. I don't blame her and forgive her her trespasses. I am an unwanted remnant from another life…one which we both wish we could forget.

My hands won't stop shaking. The gray-green mottling that comes with the infection is now past my shoulder. I don't have long, so I must keep my tale brief if it is to be told.

Again, let's return to the life and death of Abdul Jehangeer. I ask the Seraphim: Is there is a subtler way of denying this man's progeny? Render him sterile, perhaps? Cause him an accident? The Seraphim assured me that it was his influence that caused these events or variations of these events to transpire. His seed or his influence on the seed of others was the fulcrum on which the world's fate pivoted. Attempts by others to alter this man's destiny had been made, but without success. Dead, he could impregnate no one. Dead, his influence would diminish and then vanish altogether. Dead, his fate would be denied.

And so, it fell to me to kill him.

But why me, you ask? I've asked this question, too. The Seraphim cannot intervene directly. They are, after all, spiritual beings in a physical world. Their currency is influence. They can advise; they can direct, but cannot take physical action themselves. It is we, the Agents of the Seraphim, who must be God's Instruments. It is a heavy burden, but the Seraphim must not be denied.

But more to the point: The Seraphim are remarkably reticent to discuss anything but the mission or its parameters. What I do know is that there are only a chosen few in this world like me. After all, murder in the age of forensic science is a delicate matter and can only be entrusted to a chosen few. The Tree of Knowledge bore bitter fruit in that regard, I suppose. Of course, there are those who fulfill lesser assignments — whose duties don't often involve bloodletting at all. Their missions are more slight of hand...more prosaic, and, by comparison, less critical than mine. Then there are the Agents of the Seraphim. We are more the agents of last resort. Should we fail to carry out our tasks, our missions, then the world falls. My punishment for failure is to witness the catastrophe that I was unable to prevent.

It is, as you might imagine, a persuasive incentive.

Take, for example, the story of Johann Kuehberger: an Agent of the Seraphim whose failure to complete his mission caused the death of tens of millions. During the winter of 1894, Johann was given the simple task of drowning a little boy. An odious task, to be sure, but the Seraphim cannot be denied. Johann would be the only witness to the event (the Seraphim would see to that). He was given a simple mission: entice a young man out onto the thin ice of the Danube. The ice, of course, would break, the boy would drown, and the world would be denied a "terrible fate." But Johann was a compassionate man. Once the boy had fallen through the ice, and Johann heard his frantic cries, he leaped from the shore to rescue him. Sodden and nearly frozen himself, he dragged the boy to shore. After the boy was revived, Johann asked him his name.

His name was Adolf. Adolf Hitler.

Of course, Johann was not the only Agent to fail in his mission to kill Hitler. Any amateur student of history will tell you that Hitler eluded death a number of times throughout his life. Attempts were made by angelic and prosaic forces alike to no avail. However, Johann's penance for his failure was watching his world disintegrate around him, as his friends and family were rounded up and interned at one of Passau's famous concentration camps.

I am far more fortunate than Johann! I will not live much longer. God is gracious, meting out his mercy with his vengeance.

And, perhaps, God feels that I have suffered enough.

It was the revenant of Abdul Jehangeer who gave me this mission. I saw him, bloated and rotting, staring at me beneath a subway grate months after I had dismembered and disposed of his body. His abrupt appearance startled me, but I felt no fear in his presence — only exhilaration and anticipation. The roar of the subway carried the gurgling rasp of the Seraphim's voice despite the gash in Jehangeer's throat. The Seraphim warned me that the FBI had recovered forensic evidence from our encounter (a strand of my hair, I think it was) and that "the noose was tightening." No doubt, it was my imagination when I saw Jehangeer attempt a smirk at my blunder. Or perhaps I merely mistook his snarling grimace for amusement…undoubtedly the result of the pain from the destroyed musculature in his neck.

Besides, why would the Seraphim mock me?

Speaking through Jehangeer, the Seraphim instructed me to find Dr. Anna Klein, a paleoclimatologist working for the University of Washington. Dr. Klein had been studying ice cores pulled from the Ross Ice Shelf in Antarctica for nearly ten years. Her analysis of prehistoric spore distribution and preservation in the ice was highly regarded in her field (and goes to show how deeply the seeds from the Tree of Knowledge have taken root in the souls of men). Jehangeer's revenant explained that a previously unexamined core yielded a deadly surprise: a fungus that had somehow been preserved in the ice for tens of thousands of years. The fungus (which Klein would name *Ophiocordyceps Immortalis*) went extinct during the last ice age — and a good thing, too.

The spores of this fungus, once inhaled, readily germinate in the soft, damp folds of the sinus cavity. As time goes on, and the colony becomes more established, the fungus moves beyond the sinus and into the cranium, where it targets and destroys the brain's higher cognitive functions. The host's behavior becomes more and more erratic — more violent and primitive. As the infection progresses, the sinus membranes rupture a grayish green spore-filled ooze that spills out the nose, eyes, and mouth. Eventually, *Ophiocordyceps Immortalis* destroys all higher brain functions, reducing the host to a sort of quasi-sentience, whose only apparent purpose is to spread the disease. If left unchecked, an adult host can produce billions of spores before the body collapses.

Usually a bite is the most effective way to infect others, as the saliva is saturated with spores, but I have seen the gray-green bile violently vomited into the mouths and faces of the uninfected to devastating effect. The infected do not seem to be affected by pain or by injury, and they cannot be reasoned with or rehabilitated. There is no cure for this disease. It does not respond to modern medications or treatments of any kind (although, amputation can, in some cases, prevent the spread of the disease throughout the body). The fatality rate is 100 percent. But the bodies of hosts continue to function long after what we call consciousness departs the body.

I wonder if their skin ever stops burning. Perhaps this is why the infected moan so piteously.

The Seraphim tell me that Dr. Klein would not only discover *Ophiocordyceps Immortalis*, but also would become the plague's first victim. A lapse in protocol in handling the deadly fungus would result in a cataclysmic epidemic. Through her, the infection would quickly spread, devastating much of the Northwestern U.S. within the first weeks of the outbreak. Within three months, Canada and Mexico would succumb to the disease, as millions of the infected shamble across the continent looking for fresh hosts. The third-world nations would fare little better than those in the industrialized world. Quarantines would fail. Entire continents would be lost.

According to the Seraphim, this outbreak would be an "extinction level event" — and not just for our species. Most of the modern warm-blooded animals would be susceptible to the infection. The resulting epidemic would kill off roughly 85 percent of land-dwelling mammals. Those species able to survive the *Ophiocordyceps* infection would become symbiotic with the fungus and evolve into species with a singular intent. Eventually *Ophiocordyceps Immortalis* would become the only life form on Earth, having assimilated all life on land, air, and sea. And so would start a new biological epoch in earth's history. Not that there would be anyone left to document it. A kingdom of mindless fungi would reign supreme on earth until the sun turned to a cinder in the sky.

The world would suffer this fate unless I was able to prevent it.

Prosaic methods to prevent the plague had proven unsuccessful. Attempts on Dr. Klein's life and work had been made for several weeks: a fire was set in the lab where she worked (but was quickly extinguished); a drunk driver was tasked to hit her (but the accident only resulted in a broken leg); a disgruntled fast-food worker was poised to give her food poisoning (but was fired before completing his mission). Thus, the failure of the lesser Agents became my mission.

I was to eliminate the vector path of this unholy plague at the source — by any means necessary. The Seraphim told me that, at this point, the probability of preventing Dr. Klein from finding and examining the contaminated core sample was virtually nil. I would only be able to prevent the spread of the infection by killing her and destroying the contaminated core sample. There was little time to prepare, as Dr. Klein's unfortunate lab mishap would occur in the next 12 hours.

Using the monies and resources that I liberated from Jehangeer's flat, I caught the next flight to Seattle. Arriving early the next morning, I scouted the quiet, serene campus, familiarizing myself with the buildings, security, and nightly schedules in the university labs. I strolled through the fall air, a seemingly casual visitor, but in my mind, I was searching for security cameras, planning my timing and plotting escape routes. According to a schedule posted on her office door, Dr. Klein had an evening class, one of several late-night classes on campus that night. It would be easy enough to distract the university security force. A dumpster fire set on the opposite side of the campus would provide ample opportunity to eliminate Dr. Klein and destroy the infected core sample before anybody even knew she was dead. I could easily make my way back to Chicago before my "crime" was discovered.

This task, however odious and necessary, should have been routine. Simple. But, like poor Johann, my reticence has condemned the human race to this semblance of existence. How the plague started or why will never be formally debated, as humanity as we know it is doomed. My testament, and only my testament, can provide the truth that science, in all its false pride, cannot! This is my legacy. Perhaps our legacy — my legacy — lies in the notion that my very humanity was humanity's own undoing.

The science labs were dark that evening. Scattered pools of fluorescent lights burned in only a couple of classrooms across the academic quad. A brisk, wintery wind blew through the campus, and the students rushed to their respective classes or dorms without paying much attention to the twilight world around them. I slipped into one of the darkened labs next door and quietly listened to Dr. Klien's muffled lecture, the thump and click of her crutches as she moved about the classroom, her students' queries and laughter. I watched the sliver of the fall moon rise above the trees and listened at the dull wind whistling through the leaky window panes. Somewhere across campus, the smoldering bundle I had placed into a dumpster was starting to alight. A thin trail of smoke could be seen rising from behind the buildings.

It was nearly 8 p.m. before Dr. Klein dismissed her students. There were, of course a few stragglers — students, who no doubt hoped to improve their grades or clarify a talking point. I watched the last one leave, just as the dumpster fire was reaching its peak.

Klein had her back to me when I entered the room. Scattered atop her desk were various frosted containers, each swaddled in a silvery metallic blanket. These must be the core samples! She was loading them onto a small hand dolly, leaning around an ungainly set of battered crutches. She didn't hear me come in, but she did hear the door click shut behind me. Startled, she fumbled and dropped one of the containers. It shattered at her feet, spilling a steaming fragmented cylinder of greenish black ice at her feet. She turned then, and in that instant, I knew her.

Gone was the girl I knew as my sister, but Nan still had our mother's eyes. They were wide with recognition and bewilderment as she glimpsed the lead pipe clenched in my hand. I longed to rush over to her, hold her in my arms, but the Seraphim bade me pause. Already, the deadly spores from the ice core had been released! The air between us filled with a horrible miasma as they disseminated throughout the room. She whispered my name then. My true name. A tear cascaded down her cheek, falling into the quickly sublimating ice below. She gasped, taking in the noxious air, sealing her fate.

She stumbled toward me, her crutches scattering the remains of the ice core, and fell into me with the warmth of a sister's embrace. Sobbing, she clung to me, the years of childhood trauma and abuse boiling to the surface. I wept then, too. The pipe fell from my numb fingers, and I held my sister in my arms for the first time in decades.

I heard the Seraphim wail in the sirens across campus.

I stayed with Nan until the end. In her delirium, she bit me, no doubt hastening the infection that we shared. By the time the campus was quarantined, it was already too late to prevent the spread of the contamination. I should have killed her and then myself that night. I should have burned the building down, with us inside. But, instead, I held my sister and destroyed the world.

)X(X(X(X(X(X(X(X(X(X(X(

About the Author

Michael Picco conjures his tales in his dimly lit, cozy basement studio in Denver, Colorado. When he's not bathed in the glow of computer monitor, he's out wandering through the hills where you'll find him drawing or reading. He loves collecting odd clichés, making people laugh, and strong, freshly brewed coffee. Michael received his B.A. in English from Western State College in Colorado. *Fraser: The Disappearance of Michael Pitts* is his first novel-length publication (written in collaboration with Mark Clodi), and, he is currently wrapping up a collection of short stories: *Scenes from the Carnival Lounge* (expected release in 2018). He was inspired to write *Agents of the Seraphim* after reading a critical essay on schizophrenia and the role it's played in modern religions.

DICK AND RUTH FOREVER

Paul Tanner

Dick and Ruth Harmon had been married fifty years as of the end of August. The actual day of their anniversary went by with little fanfare, though not owing to a lack of gravity over the occasion. The fact was that Ruth had been in the hospital for a bladder infection a full week before the big party planned by their kids. Carl, the eldest, even lost part of the deposit he had put down on a banquet hall in Topsfield, but there were no hard feelings. Everyone understood how important it was for Ruth to recover completely, and if that meant putting off the celebration, some then so be it.

The two old lovers spent the evening of their anniversary in Ruth's hospital room, drinking white wine from little paper cups. Dick, a life-long Budweiser man, had learned over the years that the occasional concession to a woman's drink could buy a lot of favor in a marriage. He had snuck the bottle of chardonnay in. Even at seventy-eight, he was a spry devil who liked thumbing his nose at rules, especially the silly regulations of someplace like a hospital. He and his wife of half a century watched the sun lower in the sky, sharing a small strawberry cake, and chuckling at memories of some of the places where they had gotten up to funny business over the many years.

"Well, my blushing bride," he said after finishing his second cup of wine, "I've got half a mind to climb in that bed of yours right now, bladder infection or no bladder infection."

"Oh *Dick*!" She swatted at him playfully, feigning disapproval. "That shop closed up a long time ago."

"Hey, you can't blame a guy for trying." He grinned. All his front teeth were the originals. They were the color of souvenir gold nuggets, and the gums had receded over the decades, but the charm was still there, just like when they first met in 1965.

He squeezed her hand, and she squeezed back.

"My girl."

"That I am."

He nudged the linoleum chair a little closer to the bed. She slid a little closer to the edge and laid her head as best she could on his shoulder. They sat there for a long while, until finally one of the nurse's assistants had to poke her head in and tell them visiting hours were over. Even then, Dick stayed an extra ten minutes, his girl by his side.

"My Girl" was playing on the stereo the first night they actually met. It was the Christmas party for Nolan Tool and Die, where they both worked — she as a member of the small secretarial pool and he as an apprentice machinist. They had gotten a look at each other in the couple of months since Dick started there, and though intrigued by him, Ruth had also noticed that he was different from the other boys in the shop. His hair, for one thing, in contrast with their crew cuts and flattops, was sculpted in a shiny black pompadour. It reminded Ruth of the toughs who used to start fights in the parking lot outside of ball games when she was in junior high. He didn't seem that way, though. For one thing, he kept mainly to himself. When the other apprentices went our for beers at the end of a Friday shift, tagging along with the journeymen and telling dirty jokes meant for the secretaries to hear, Dickey was never with them. He stayed behind, tidying up his station. There was something...*sensitive* about him that Ruth couldn't quite place. Not that he seemed soft. He was intense, too, and the few times he had looked at her, she was almost...she didn't want to use the word intimidated — that was too strong — but *impressed* by his intensity. He had eyes like a wolf.

The party was held in a VFW hall just beyond the city limits. Ruth went with a couple of charmless girls named Jeanine and Kathy, who made up half of the secretarial pool. The fourth girl, Cindy, was married to a jealous type who gave her the occasional black eye. This meant she wasn't allowed to go to parties, Christmas or otherwise.

Ruth had been the one to drive, while Jeanine and Kathy exchanged vicious gossip along with a bottle of peppermint schnapps. They offered Ruth some, but she declined. The stuff gave her heartburn, and besides, she was half afraid of showing up tipsy to an event where the two brothers who owned the company, Jack and Billy Nolan, would doubtless be watching their employees for improprieties. Well, Billy would be watching the girls at least. Ruth had been raised with principles. The fact that her boss was a drunken letch didn't change that.

Coming into the VFW, she had been left almost immediately alone by her so-called friends, who disappeared in the vicinity of the mistletoe where a few unsavory-looking shop hands stood around with bad posture, smoking languidly. The boys looked up with revived cheer when the office girls arrived. Ruth immediately regretted then not taking at least a little dose of the schnapps, if for no other reason than to calm her nerves in this crowd of people she either didn't much know or else didn't much like. The rough men who operated the machines all seemed to be in attendance. A few appeared to have brought along their wives, because in one corner stood a gaggle of women overdressed for a place with plywood floors. They seemed to be looking at Ruth and leaning in a little closer to say something unpleasant. *To hell with them,* she didn't feel guilty for thinking. Maybe she was a few pounds heavier than she might be, and at twenty-four, she was unmarried, but she was the one to draw looks from men and boys wherever she went. Having developed early and well — so much so that the junior high gym teacher Mr. Wetherill had to be reassigned on her account — she was used to male attention. Her eyes were the color of palm, and she had hair the shade of a blood orchid.

What she wanted was to go to the bar and get a little nip of something, just to take the edge off. A girl couldn't do a think like that in a place like this. Not even a half pint of beer. Not with all those men around the bar, some of them already leering. It was horrible. People in general were.

It was then that she felt a hand on her shoulder. She turned, and there was that black hair and those eyes. She hadn't noticed his teeth before, but she did now. They were straight and white, and the way the lips curled up on one side made him look like Marlon Brando.

"You know who I am?" His voice was deeper than she expected.

"Of course."

"I been keeping an eye on you."

She didn't know what to say to something like that.

"You ain't like these other girls," he said. He nodded his head in the direction of the gossiping women in the corner.

"Does that mean you're different from the other boys?" She looked toward the louts around the bar. "You noticing a thing like that?"

"Might be I am," he said.

Ruth had noticed the music when she first came in, but as soon as he started talking, it went away. His eyes were like a hypnotist's. They bore right into her.

"You don't mind nigger music?" he said.

She gave him a look.

"You know," he jerked his thumb in the direction of the speakers set up at the back of the room. "This Motown stuff."

"I guess I hadn't thought of it one way or the other. It's just music."

"Naw, it's nigger music. But it's all right with me. I don't care what anybody says, those spades can put together a pretty good tune."

She wasn't used to this kind of talk. Her father wasn't prejudiced, for one thing. He also didn't care about music one way or another. He occasionally put on a warped Perry Como record when some of his old army buddies came over to play cards.

The record changed, and Smokey Robinson and the Miracles came on with "Tracks of My Heart."

"You dance?" he said.

She shook her head.

"I didn't think so. Me neither. We've got that in common."

"I've got two left feet," she said.

"How about drink? You do that?"

"No. But you might be able to convince me just this once." At the first note of the Smokey Robinson tune, a few of the men from the bar and a few of the women from the gossip circle had found each other and made their way onto the plywood dance floor for the ritual of lumbering through the number one hit of the week. He grabbed her hand and led her in the direction of the bar.

"We don't even know each other," she said in half-protest. He stopped and turned to look at her. Those eyes. She felt a flutter.

"We do now."

He wasn't like the other boys.

She felt as if hours had gone by but saw when she looked at the clock above the bar that it had been less than half of one. The red and green of the Narragansett Beer logo emblazoned on the clock swam a little. *Christmas colors,* she thought dreamily. The room was fuzzy in her peripheral vision, and the music and voices were a dull blur of sounds, like crowd noise in a dream, or something heard from underwater. It *was* almost as if he were hypnotizing her. His voice was low and syrupy, and he repeated many of the same words it seemed, and they were pretty words, almost too nice for a boy from Lowell, Massachusetts, who'd left school early to join the Marine Corps. He wasn't educated, but he seemed to choose the things he said in a way she had never heard anyone do before. He was kind, but he dealt smiles out sparingly, like rewards for a dog he was teaching a new trick. He was cool. Marlon Brando again. James Dean. Not as Hollywood handsome, of course — he had a scar that ran along his chin and a street fighter's bludgeoned nose — but cool, nonetheless. She found herself a little in awe of him. He no longer seemed like an apprentice or even the kind of person who'd ever set foot in VFW Post 29. More like a poet maybe, riding a motorcycle across the Western desert, or a hustler who a society woman might take as her lover. Ruth blushed at the thought. Maybe it was the gin and tonic. She could feel the color in her cheeks and on her neck. She hoped she didn't seem drunk. Just how much gin had the bartender put into her drink?

"...an innocent." He was finishing a sentence she couldn't recall the beginning of.

"Innocent?"

"You are."

"An innocent?"

"A babe in the woods. A child."

"I'm no child."

"I don't know about that. I'm thinking maybe I shouldn't have bought you that drink. I wouldn't want to get in any trouble with the authorities."

She was charmed. At twenty-four, she practically felt like an old maid. The flattery made her a little giddier. Everything was going to her head tonight.

"I'll have you know I'm a grown woman."

"You still live with your folks, though."

"Maybe I do; maybe I don't."

"You do. What are you going to tell me? You room with those two slobs you came in with?"

Jeanine and Kathy. Where had they gone off to? Necking with the boys from the mistletoe? In a car? One in the front seat, the other in the back? All that breathing from all those people in that little space. She felt a tingle, a rush of warmth, though this time not to her head. This was bad. *Bad bad bad.* If her father had even an inkling of the kind of company she was keeping at the moment, he'd...

She didn't want to think about him now, didn't want him associated in any way with the various tingles and buzzing she was experiencing. He could stay home with his Perry Como records and his whiskey and have himself a ball. She was an adult. A fully grown one.

Just beyond the bar, she noticed someone move and though the figure was fuzzy, she could tell right away it was Billy Nolan. He'd been watching her, she realized suddenly. On some level, she had sensed a pair of eyes fixed on her, but Dickey's stare had been so intense that it blotted everything else out. It was like the gravitational pull of a planet compared to one of its moons. Now Billy was coming in their direction. He weaved a little as he did, his big red face a child's balloon in breeze.

"Here comes the boss. Stand up straight and look busy," Dickey said.

Billy seemed to be doing his best to focus on them, but his gaze went in and out. On the way, he half-tripped over someone's foot and cocked a fist back in the instinctual pose of the barroom brawler. He caught himself, exaggerated the fist as if the whole thing was a joke, and gave the other guy a big jocular slap on the back. The boss said something in a loud voice, probably a promise to buy the next round.

"Shit canned," Dickey said, touching her shoulder conspiratorially. She felt the rough pads of his fingers through the cashmere of her sweater, making the skin there sing. "Three sheets to the wind."

Billy had made it to them now, huffing a little with the effort. He grinned idiotically.

"Well, what do we have here?" he said. His words slid around some. "A couple of my employees sharing a cup of Christmas cheer?" He reached in the direction of Ruth and clumsily wrestled the drink from her hand. He held it up toward the fluorescent lights above and examined the contents. Some of the liquid sloshed out as he did. His other hand found its way to the small of her back and began circling in little concentric patterns like he was her prom date. The warm singing dissipated right away. Instead, she felt the chill of gooseflesh.

She thought of the night back in October when she had stayed late to do inventory. She remembered the reflection of headlights through the tiny window of the stock room. A few minutes later, she had heard the squeak of hinges from one of the side doors. Her heart was beating a mile a minute, she recalled. All that fall and the preceding summer, girls had gone missing in the area. Three in total. The last, Margaret McGonegal, had disappeared earlier that month. The poor girl had lived only a couple of miles from Nolan Tool and Die. A missing poster with Margaret's face was even pinned to the corkboard in the break room. As these panicked thoughts galloped through her head, Ruth had heard the door of the stock room open and there had been Billy Nolan, leaning into the room, grinning stupidly just like he did tonight. Alcohol had wafted off of him like paint thinner or turpentine, detectable intermittently. Just like tonight.

Dickey had taken his own hand away from where it sat on her shoulder and gathered it in half a fist at his side. There was something conspiratorial about this, just as when he had touched her shoulder.

"And one of my most reliable employees here," Billy said, slapping a hand in the vicinity of Dickey's back. He just grazed it. "A real meticulous kind of guy. Always keeps his station ship-shape."

Dickey's face betrayed nothing. Not even an eye twitched. James Dean. Marlon Brando.

"Fucking meticulous as hell," Billy said. "Practically never seen anybody like that outside the Navy. You serve, Harmon?"

Dickey's face still didn't move, aside from a flicker of his eyes in the direction of his superior. "Marine Corps. 2nd Battalion, 4th Regiment," he said, pausing for a beat, "sir."

"*Sir.* I like that. Shows respect. Cute. As a Navy man, I guess I'd feel disrespected if you called me anything besides sir. The Marine Corps is a branch of the Navy, after all," he said. "The Marines are the goddamned grunts who do all the dirty work. Crawling through mud, that kind of shit."

"Yes, sir." The clenched fist balled a little tighter, like a winch. Ruth noticed, though Billy didn't seem to. He was pretty well past noticing much of anything.

"You know what the real sign of respect was in the Navy?"

"Sir?"

"The real show of respect," said Billy, his hand moving from the small of Ruth's back to her hip, "happened on shore leave."

"Shore leave," said Dickey.

"Yeah, when the guys were on liberty."

"Liberty."

"Shopping for whores. They'd all go into town to get a look at the local product. Haggle prices. You know the drill."

Dickey was quiet.

"The ultimate sign of respect was when a young stud from the ship managed to get himself a real good whore. If a commanding officer came on the scene and saw the two strutting arm in arm, the sailor would give his whore to the officer."

Ruth squirmed away from Billy now, but he tightened his grip. He pulled her against him, and she could feel his penis, hard through his pants. His breath was hot on her neck.

"Keep in mind, as officers we had all kinds of duties to perform on board before we could take our leave. It was only fair that we got the top-shelf pussy. Everybody understood that. It's a shame more people don't today." Billy's hand had been traveling upward as he talked, moving from Ruth's hip to her ribs, and now it cupped her right breast.

She pulled away from him again, this time managing to get away. She looked to Dickey, as if this stranger could protect her. The expression on his face wasn't one of anger or of embarrassment either. She couldn't read it. Something was going on in that head of his. Wheels were turning. Ruth was sure her own face glowed like the red lights on the little Christmas tree behind the bar. *Thump-thump-thump-thump* went her heart. She really wished she hadn't had that drink, or that the bartender hadn't put all that gin in it, or whatever it was he had spiked it with.

"What's the matter?" said Billy. "I say the wrong thing?"

"Dickey was just going to take me home," she said suddenly, surprising herself.

"Take you home, is he? Nice church-going girl like you?"

"*Drop* me home."

"But you just got here," he said. "I never even got a dance."

Before he could say anything else, Ruth found herself reaching for Dickey's hand. It was still clenched in a fist. *Tonight was just full of surprises*, she thought to herself. Another surprise: the fist softened slightly at her touch, rough fingers yielding some to her own. Opening. Their fingertips touched then entwined. She pulled him in the direction of the door and he followed. The faces of the men around the bar turned with them, some with raised eyebrows, a few even letting out wolf whistles and drunken cheers. The women shot poisonous looks from their corner.

Ruth turned, once, on the way out the door. Her boss stood alone in the crowd, swaying a little, looking as if he had just been told a joke whose punch line he didn't understand.

XXXX

The air outside was cold and clear. She expected the night chill to have a sobering effect, but somehow it was the opposite. Walking out into the darkness was disorienting. Not much used to walking in heels, she stumbled. Dickey caught her. He held her a moment longer than necessary.

"You're a cheap date," he said. "Barely half a drink, and you're ready for bed."

"That was some half of a drink. And I thought you were a gentleman."

"I never said anything about being one of those."

"Well you'd better be, if you want the privilege of driving me home."

"You got a car here, don't you?"

"It's Kathleen's. I just said I'd drive."

"How do you know I'm not some kind of weirdo?" He cocked his head a little, looking at her with half a grin.

"My womanly intuition tells me you're not."

"For all you know, I could be the creep who's been kidnapping those girls."

"You're a mystery man, but not that kind of mystery," she said. "The good kind."

"Well, let's go then." He jutted his chin in the direction of a car on the edge of the lot, a large sedan, funeral black in the moonlight. It was older than most of the other cars and trucks in the lot, its bulbous hood and roof out of step with the sleek angles of the newer vehicles. Still, it looked powerful. The word menacing came to mind, but she almost immediately thought of how silly that was. If anything, Dickey was harmless compared to a lot of the other machinists and die makers in the shop. There was Butch St. Jacques, for one, who came in every couple of Mondays with skinned red knuckles and a shiner or two. There were the Murphy boys, three brothers who once spent a weekend in the drunk tank after brawling with an entire engine company of the Lowell Fire Department. Then, of course, there was Billy Nolan.

Dickey was sensitive. As if to prove her thoughts correct, he opened the door for her and caught her a second time when she nearly fell getting into the passenger seat. Maybe she hadn't eaten a hearty enough supper. After all, she was dieting, practically eating like a rabbit. That was the only explanation that made sense. She never got like this.

"You stay here. I've got something I need to do. Won't take more than a couple minutes."

Before Ruth could say anything, he had eased to door shut and was gone. She went to look in the rearview mirror and realized there wasn't one. The car bounced on its shocks, and she could hear the noises of rummaging in what must have been the trunk. Then there was a slam. Footsteps. Where was he going? What errand could be so pressing in the cold parking lot of the Christmas party? She closed her eyes. The lure of sleep worked on her like a dark current. She tried to open them once, but it was no use. She sunk deeper and deeper until she had sunk all the way.

When she opened her eyes again, the car was in motion, and she couldn't move her arms. A weight pressed down on her, and for a moment, she felt panic well up in her chest, moving into her throat.

"Morning, Sleeping Beauty," Dickey said.

She turned her head to look at him, blinked a few times. He was steering with one hand, the other hand twirling a strand of her hair. It occurred to her then why she couldn't move her arms. He had laid his heavy wool pea coat over her. The thing had to weigh ten pounds.

"Morning?" She looked out the window at the dark road.

"It's 12:30. Sunday morning."

"How long have we been driving?"

"Couple of hours."

"A couple of *hours*?"

"I couldn't bring you home in the condition you were in. That wouldn't have been very gentlemanly of me, now would it?"

"But where are we now?"

"Just outside town. I've been sticking to the county roads. I do a lot of driving."

"Just driving?"

"And thinking some." He took his eyes off the road long enough to look at her.

"What about?"

"Different things. You, mainly." Eyes back on the road.

She felt herself blush.

Neither of them said anything for a long while. He took her to a lonesome place on a hill overlooking the lights of Lowell. It was a lover's lane or a lover's leap. Maybe both.

When they made love, that, too, was wordless. The car's interior wasn't suited for it. She felt springs digging into her skin through the threadbare upholstery of the seats. Also, he hurt her, big as he turned out to be, and surprisingly rough. The music that played at low volume on the car's stereo was all rhythm it seemed, all percussion, and his movements were in synch with it. Faster, then slower. Faster again.

There was one song whose melody she could make out. An ascending guitar line floated through the fog of drink and sleep and through the exterior hum of pain. Despite all of it, the words came through, too. It was the Temptations again. *My Girl.*

The music did something to her. Where at first whatever pleasure there had been was spiked with a lot of pain, that song and his labors worked together like an aesthetic. She opened her eyes and saw his were open, too. They were so beautiful, it almost hurt to look into them. Flecks of gold shone even in the darkness. They were sunshine, not on a cloudy day but in the dead of a winter night. All at once it, was the month of May.

She woke in her own bed, in her father's house, with only a vague memory of having gotten there. Dickey, of course, was gone. The physical memory of him remained as a throbbing between her legs that would last a full day.

Ruth was unsure of how she would make it through Saturday and Sunday without some contact with him. She felt like a schoolgirl who just might desperately languish by the phone waiting for his call. The problem was that she had never even given him her number.

Looking out her bedroom window, the glare of daylight sent shards of pain into her temples and the backs of her eyeballs. Her father was in the yard, wearing his red-and-black checked wool jacket. His lumberjack shirt, she had always thought as a girl. He was hauling a wheelbarrow full of wood from the enormous pile at the edge of the property. Knowing him, he'd be at it for hours, dragging load after load to the bulkhead that he would then stack down in the basement. This meant she could safely get in and out of the shower without their paths crossing.

She pulled herself out of bed. The room was itself, yet somehow alien. The dimensions felt stilted, distorted. She went to put her feet in the fuzzy bunny slippers she had worn since high school. They were tattered and the pink of the ears had long since faded to grey, but they were more comfortable than anything else she owned.

Most of the time she located them by feel, fishing them out from under the bed with her toes. She felt around, locating nothing but dust bunnies. Dropping to her knees, also sore from one of the positions she'd found herself in the night before, she winced for a moment, then felt a rush of pleasure at the memory. The slippers were nowhere to be found, though. Strange. Everything was, it seemed lately.

That was when the phone rang. The shrill trilling echoed violently through the empty hall. The phone itself sat on a small table between the bathroom and the room where her father slept.

It rang a second time. Even though she should have been expecting it, Ruth jumped. Her heart pounded. There was a throbbing in her temples, something new and distinct from her hangover.

Dickey! a part of her mind sang. Dare she wish something so sweet?

By the third ring, she had made her way shuddering and breathless to the phone.

"Hello?" she said in a voice not entirely her own.

"Ruth," the voice was female.

"Yes?"

"It's Kathy."

Her heart sunk. She was silent for what felt like a long time.

"Ruth? Honey? Are you there?"

"Yes."

"Have you heard the news?"

"News?"

"About Billy? I mean Mr. Nolan. Oh Jesus!" Kathy began to sob on the other end of the line. There was an air of theater about this, like it was something she had practiced.

"What..." Ruth began, then stopped. She thought again of the night in the stock room. She thought of him the night before at the Christmas party. "What about him?"

"I hate to be the one to tell you," said Kathy, "but Mr. Nolan died last night." There was more muffled sobbing.

"What do you mean died?" Her heart — deflated just seconds before by the realization that it was Kathy calling instead of Dickey — started to beat fast again.

"Oh, it's just so awful," sobbed Kathy. "Car wreck. On the way home from the party. He was only thirty-nine!"

Ruth was wide-awake now, her hangover evaporated like a morning fog burned away by the sun. She still felt funny, most of her body numb from shock. There was one part that she became suddenly aware of, though: her face. It had pulled itself into a grin. She smiled and smiled for a long time after confessing her grief to Kathy and hanging up the phone.

It took a while for things to get back to normal at Nolan Tool and Die, though eventually, they did. The official police statement was that William Edward Nolan, aged thirty-nine, businessman, had met his end on an icy stretch of State Road 110 where there also happened to be a wicked blind curve. His vehicle, a candy apple red 1964 Buick Riviera, took a nosedive into the Merrimack River and never came back up. Speculation and rumor had it that drink was involved, though such information never made it into any official report. The first cops on the scene the early morning of the accident reported that there weren't even any tire marks; it seemed the poor bastard had met his end without even a chance to hit the brakes.

The other brother, Jack, took over more of the day-to-day responsibilities than he ever had before Billy's untimely death. Jack had always been the reserved one of the pair, leaving the work of management and employee relations to his more outgoing, boisterous brother. After an initial period of shock and grieving, though, he really came into his own. He gave up some of the quixotic tasks Billy had occupied himself with: eliminating employee drinking at lunch (a policy that had most certainly never applied to management); getting to the bottom of who was routinely stealing tools from the work benches of various employees; figuring out who in the hell had stashed the carcass of a twenty-pound carp behind the boiler in retribution for God knew what slight, real or imagined. This last thing had bordered on obsession for Billy, who interrogated employees at random in his office as if he were a detective, combining good cop and bad cop in an industrial version of Dr. Jekyll and Mr. Hyde. Jack didn't concern himself with this demented prank. He focused instead on making the company profitable. It worked. Within a year, Nolan Tool and Die found it necessary to hire half a dozen new employees. Business boomed.

Things boomed for Dickey and Ruth, too. Or maybe bloomed was more accurate. After the Christmas party, they were known as an item around the shop. They were seen everywhere together, climbing in and out of his Rocket 88 on the way to and from work, driving the roads in and around town. When the weather warmed, they were spotted at the soda fountains and hamburger stands of Lowell. Dickey was the perfect gentleman he had never promised to be. Ruth's devotion grew by the day

He initiated her into things she had never had the courage to dream, opened whole worlds for her, both abstract and concrete. Love. Lust. Adventure. Danger. Poetry. Philosophy. He gave them all to her. Just her. Had there been other girls? Sure, plenty. They were all in the past, though. He snapped his fingers, and they were gone. When she rested her head on his chest — in the car, or his bed, or in a newly turned field with dark soil loose beneath their heaving bodies, the kind of oddball romantic place he sometimes took her — she could feel his heart beat, and it was always steady as a metronome. She was his girl. He would say so sometimes out of the blue: "My girl." He didn't need to, though. She knew.

He proposed in May of that first year. It was in one of his fields, actually, an out-of-the-way place he liked to drive her from time to time. He took her suddenly, on top of the new alfalfa at the edge, heaving and thrusting with wild abandon, rutting almost like an animal. Afterward, he got down on one knee and presented her with a ring that glittered like something out of Fort Knox. Where on earth he had gotten such a treasure, and how he afforded it, she never asked. She just said yes, and kept saying it for a long time afterward.

Eventually, Ruth got over the bladder infection. With a little help from a husband with the patience of a saint, three terrific kids, not to mention seven even more terrific grandkids and a visiting nurse who came to the house three times weekly, she managed a full recovery. Before too long, she was back to her weekly game of Bridge, along with volunteering in the special ed pre-school whose students she thought of both privately and publicly as lighting up her week every Tuesday and Thursday.

It was a Saturday afternoon, several weeks after Ruth's return to health, when Dick suggested they take a drive in the country. It was mid-September and the daytime temperatures hovered in the sixties. The trees had yet to explode in the crimson fires of autumn that were so spectacular in this part of New England. Still, the relentless green of the canopy mirrored precisely the weather in that long-ago May when they had first been engaged. The air smelled exactly the way it had then.

They even had the Rocket 88 to ride in. It wasn't *the* Rocket 88, of course; the original had long since been sold. This was another that Dick had bought and restored a few years back, after finally retiring from Nolan Tool and Die with forty years of service. With time on his hands, he had scoured auctions and newspaper ads throughout the region, finally settling on a model that mimicked the car of his youth. He had painstakingly restored every detail, down to the matte black finish. It now sat in the garage and was brought out a few times a year for cruise nights and the occasional country drive.

He held the door for her again, just like their first night together, though this time in gentle consideration of her birdlike old lady's bones. She was just as grateful as she had been the first time.

First they drove into town. So much had changed. Most of the old soda fountains and hamburger stands were gone. There was one place down near the river that still sold soft-serve ice cream. Forty-eight flavors were advertised on a brightly painted wooden sign. It also served hamburgers and hot dogs, and if you sat at one of the brightly painted picnic tables, eventually a girl would come out to take your order. These waitresses, if you could call them that, were all high school- or college-aged, wore their hair in ponytails or braids, and dressed in tight, cut-off jean shorts.

Dick and Ruth sat at an electric blue picnic table and licked at their cones. "See something else on the menu you like?" Ruth said, nodding in the direction of the girl hustling past them with a tray.

"What?" Dick shrugged, playing ignorant, "What'd I do?"

Ruth swatted at him playfully with her handbag. "It's not what you did, Buster, it's what you *thought*. After fifty years, I can see right into your mind."

"Hey, just because I'm on a diet doesn't mean I can't look at the menu!"

She swatted him again.

When they had finished their cones, Dick helped Ruth up from the bench and guided her carefully to the car. He eased her into the passenger seat and gave her the peck on the cheek, then went around to the passenger side and fired the ignition.

They hadn't gone half a block when Dick turned to her and said, "How'd you like to do something we haven't done together in years?"

"Together? Give me a hint," Ruth said.

"I don't think you need any hints," Dick said. "Think of our signature thing."

"I think I know exactly what you mean," she said, eyes shining like new dimes.

"I drive?"

"I talk."

Their hands met, entwined.

They rolled along at considerably less than the speed limit. If they had been on a main road, someone would have surely been behind them, laying on the horn and giving creative hand signals in their rear view. These, however, were side streets that dead-ended by the river. Nothing ever happened in places like this. It was twenty minutes before they saw anything. Finally, after a number of fruitless turns, heading down toward the river then back in the direction of the highway, it was Ruth who noticed her.

She was walking a tiny dog, a little terrier that stopped to shiver every few feet. The girl appeared to be in her early twenties. She wore her hair loose, and it hung midway down her back.

When Dick and Ruth pulled up next to her, she turned her head with such a lack of awareness, such an innocent oblivion about her face, that it nearly seemed wrong to address her. It was almost like addressing the face of a doll.

"Excuse us, sweetheart," Ruth said, "but we seem to be all turned around."

"You're lost?" the girl said. A furrow of concern appeared on her face.

"I'm afraid so," said Ruth. She clutched a map. "Routes 110 and 113 and 495 and just plain 95. It all gets so confusing."

The girl laughed politely. "Well, let me see if I can help you get back on track." She leaned the top half of her body into the passenger seat, looking down at the map, and that was when Dick struck with the Taser. She jerked like a marionette, legs kicking behind her and her torso, which still hung through the window. That was when he brought the blackjack down on top of her skull. In the old days ,he would have used a ligature, but his reflexes were not what they used to be and he could no longer risk it.

The first blow stunned her, and her eyes crossed like an actress playing slapstick. The second blow was directly to her face, loosing a couple teeth and stifling any protest. Her mouth was a blur of red.

No more slapstick. The rest was quick. It came back instantly, like riding a bicycle or sex. Once initiated, a person never really forgot.

Afterward, when it was all done, the couple lay together in the field they had come back to so many times over the years. They lounged on a red-checked picnic blanket in one of its far corners. Beneath the blanket was freshly turned earth.

They both had arthritis, not to mention her artificial hip and his bum knee, all of which would make getting up off the hard ground a challenge. They were in no hurry, though. Plenty of daylight remained, and a familiar song floated to them from the car stereo. They had left it running, volume knob turned up all the way. *Oldies 101* was playing The Temptations. It was the month of May all over again.

)O()O()O()O()O()O()O()O(

About the Author

Paul Tanner lives in Rhode Island with his wife and two small children, less than a mile from H.P. Lovecraft's grave. By day, he teaches elementary school; by night, he writes tales of horror and dark suspense that the school board would most likely disapprove of. His recent work has appeared in the *Flash Fiction Offensive, Massacre Magazine, HelloHorror,* and several anthologies.

HE SMELLED LIKE SMOKE

Tiffany Michelle Brown

The little boy with a lick of haystack-colored hair and rosy cheeks was covered in leeches from head to toe. Beneath his shirt, they squiggled and squirmed and grew fat on blood. I had a fleeting thought the boy looked more like a gelatin mold, a great throbbing, writhing mass, than a human being.

The boy didn't seem to notice, sucking his thumb and looking around the plane cabin with the excitement and the naiveté of the young. I waited in anticipation for one of the gluttonous leeches, the one clinging to the boy's neck, to pop.

His mother, a woman with a gunshot wound still smoking on the side of her head, picked up the little boy, sat him in his seat, and strapped the seatbelt across his lap. She paid no heed to the bulbous worms fixed to his belly — and well, everywhere.

I sighed and closed my eyes, clutching the strap of my carry-on bag a little tighter in my right hand. I counted slowly to ten, imagining the sleepy ocean off the coast of Maui creeping up onto the shore and then recessing into foam. When I opened my eyes, the leeches were gone. The gunshot wound was gone. The man behind me cleared his throat, an indication that I was holding up the line of passengers boarding the plane.

I found my seat, 14B, and slid in. I took a small, slim journal out of my carry-on and wrote down everything I could remember about my vision of the little boy and his mother. The gruesome details would come in handy the next time I was on set.

While I reviewed my scribbled notes, a man slinked into the seat next to me, a whisper of pressed cotton.

He smelled like smoke. Not the kind from cigarettes that sits in your clothes and reminds you of subways, but the kind from campfires — thick and rich like pine and ghost stories.

I shifted in my seat and straightened my skirt to lean in a little closer to him. I lowered my eyes and took a discreet, albeit long inhale. As the smell of camping trips washed over me, I thought of three things — s'mores, cold beer, and sex under the stars. I imagined his thick, blond hair tangled in my hands, and it was enough to make me shudder.

I let a lazy grin sweep across my face — until I realized the woman across the aisle was staring at me. She shot me a smirk and raised an eyebrow. Blood rushed to my cheeks and burned beneath my skin. I sat back in my seat, folded my hands in my lap, and closed my eyes, mortified.

That's what you get for smelling a complete stranger in public, I thought.

"Headache?"

He spoke. Pine needles. Kindling. *Pop.*

I took a deep breath. "Yeah, something like that."

"I hate flying, too," the man said.

I turned my head and was tempted to call him a liar. His broad shoulders, encased in a crisp gray suit, were buoyant but relaxed by his sides. The solid bank of his chest rose and fell in a steady, subdued rhythm. His eyes, the color of candied ginger and lemongrass, gazed directly into mine and didn't shift a millimeter when I swallowed audibly. He was still as a gargoyle and exhibited the same grace and stature. I suppressed the urge to lick his face.

"I've already had a cocktail," I confessed.

"Just one?" he asked.

I nodded. "In the terminal."

"I'm Jared," the man said, extending a hand with long fingers and well-manicured nails. His skin against mine made my pulse dive into my stomach.

Sizzle. Burn. Smolder.

"Alexa," I said.

"Alexa," he repeated.

Keeping his eyes on mine, Jared reached up and hit the flight attendant call button. When his gaze became overbearing, I stared down at my black skirt and wished I'd shaved my legs that morning.

A tired-looking woman in uniform with a chignon barely holding to the back of her head came over. She put one hand on the headrest in front of Jared and the other on her hip. "Can I help you, sir?"

"I was hoping to get a pre-flight shot for my friend, Alexa, here," Jared said. "Flying doesn't agree with her."

"It's against federal regulation to serve beverages before takeoff, sir," the flight attendant recited. "We'll come through the cabin to take orders later."

She took a step away, but Jared caught her hand in his. The flight attendant did a quick about face, a frown creasing her tan skin. "Sir…" she began, but she didn't finish her sentence. The crinkle between her brows melted. She breathed in deeply through her nose as if she were standing in the cold, crisp air of a forest instead of a cramped cabin that smelled like sweaty, disgruntled, tired people. Her eyes bored into Jared's and she started to look…aroused?

"Whiskey, neat," Jared said.

"Of course." The flight attendant's voice held the quality of warm maple syrup. She turned and strode off in her orthopedic shoes, apparently to get us some liquor.

Jared settled back into his seat, coolly and slowly, smiling.

"Thank you?"

"Why the question mark?"

"I'm not sure what just happened," I said.

"I asked for something. And I got it."

I didn't know what to say to that. I took an in-flight magazine out of the seat back pocket in front of me and flipped aimlessly through the pages.

The flight attendant returned a moment later with plastic cups, each filled with a thimbleful of whiskey. Jared's long fingers wrapped around the plastic. "Thank you…Debbie," he said, glancing at her nametag. Debbie walked off without a word.

Jared held out one of the cups to me. I could smell the smokiness of the whiskey. I imagined oak barrels and the forest and a hand up my skirt. I mentally swatted myself in the face. *Stop thinking about sex.*

Jared and I tipped back our glasses, and the first sip burned my throat and then coiled in my stomach. It expanded, coated my insides, and I felt my shoulders relax.

"Much better," Jared remarked.

"Yes," I said. "Thank you."

"You're welcome."

Jared took a pack of matches out of the breast pocket of his suit and let the pack flip and amble over his knuckles until our pilot announced it was time for takeoff. For some reason, I felt safe.

At 35,000 feet, I told Jared that given the choice of any tools and the right circumstances, I would kill him with razor sharp cookie cutters.

He laughed, a deep and earthy sound. "You're very…creative."

"Work hazard, I'm afraid. If the deaths were all the same in horror films, people would stop watching them. There wouldn't be any suspense or surprise," I replied.

I felt Jared's eyes on me. I turned and looked at him. My heart raced. "It's a good thing, the death I picked for you," I babbled. "It's different, interesting. I save the creativity for people I like."

"And if you didn't like me?" His smile was like the moon, all lit up and entrancing.

"It would be a cliché blow to the head with a tire iron or a crowbar." I took a sip of my cocktail. We were drinking gin now, liquid Christmas. My body was loose, and my cheeks hurt from smiling. Our conversation had been steady and playful since takeoff.

"How long have you been in Hollywood now?" Jared asked.

"Five years," I said. "Too long."

"I've always liked L.A.," Jared said. "Shiny, slick, dirty."

"And that's charming to you?"

"In a strange way, yes."

We smiled at each other. Our conversation took a natural pause, and I glanced out the window. It was sunset, and the clouds were painted a fierce and fiery magenta, their edges a ruddy blue in the shadows. The plane's engine hummed an electric lullaby.

If our conversation waned, perhaps I'd sleep. Slip off into the quieter parts of my brain, an activity that was usually unheard of for me on a plane. This was the most calm I'd ever been on a flight.

"Where are you from, Jared?"

"The other side of the world," he said.

"Mm. East Coast then."

Jared flicked me a smile. He shifted in his seat, a move that looked cool and choreographed, and his pinky finger brushed mine beneath the arm rest. He let his hand linger between us.

"Where would you go if you could go anywhere in the world right now?" Jared asked. He swished gin around in his mouth and swallowed. His hand crept over mine like the clouds crept over the sun outside. I had to cross my legs.

"Hmm," I murmured, shifting in my seat. "You know, you'd think I'd want to go somewhere calming. When I get stressed out, I think about islands, water, suntan lotion."

"St. Martin is spectacular," Jared said.

"But I think I'd get restless," I said. "There are only so many beach reads a girl can devour in her lifetime." I paused. "I'd miss the bustle, the excitement, the rudeness of a big city."

"So you'd want to go somewhere like Tokyo or New York then?"

I considered this for a moment. "Yes."

"Adventures."

"I like those."

Jared set down his drink and turned his torso to face me. I turned to mirror him, and my ears burned. The symmetry of Jared's features reminded me of the numerous statues I'd studied in college during a required art history class. But in that moment, I couldn't remember the name of a single piece of art or its creator, not while looking at the freckle under Jared's eye, skin smooth as marble, the glints of gold in his hair.

Glow. Glimmer. *Flash.*

My plastic cup suddenly felt heavy, and I set it down. Jared's fingers interlaced with mine between our seats, and a flash of heat shot through my arm. My skin began to tingle at my clavicle. The buzz spread across my shoulders and then tickled my upper back, swept low to dip down into the ridges of my hips. I imagined gentle fingertips gliding across my skin. Jared's fingertips.

"How are you feeling?" Jared asked.

"Really good," I said. My voice was breathy.

"Gin always helps."

I smiled. I knew it wasn't the gin.

"So, I have an idea," Jared said. "Alexa."

He seemed to like my name. "Yes?"

"Can I take you somewhere?"

"Of course," I said. And I meant it. This man could take me anywhere.

Jared reached over the arm rest and pushed the button on my seatbelt to release the strap. I glanced down at my lap and then smiled at Jared, shaking my head. "Who are you?"

Jared simply laughed and unhooked his own belt. Our hands unclasped as he slid out into the aisle, but my skin continued to feel warm despite the absence of his fingers. The main overhead lights in the cabin were off. Jared was instantly enveloped in shadows, but his amber eyes glowed in the darkness, beacons of light for me to follow.

I made my way into the aisle. Jared took my hand — *bubble, burn, crisp* — and we started toward the front of the plane.

Within a few steps, I started to wonder if this was a bad idea. Passengers who weren't asleep or absorbed in reading materials eyed us curiously. A man snorted to my left; a woman rolled her eyes to my right. The attention was sobering. I felt the last licks of alcohol drain from my system as if through a sieve. I took a deep breath through my nose.

"Do you know the captain or something?" I asked Jared's back. I could hear the nerves in my voice.

"Ignore them," Jared responded, sweet as molasses.

"Are you sure we should be doing this…whatever *this* is?"

"I thought you liked adventures. And you wanted to come with me."

"I do. I did," I answered.

"Then, trust me."

We stopped just outside the airplane bathroom. Jared turned to face me, and I was cloaked in the smell of campfire again. I closed my eyes, smiled, and imagined smoke rising off Jared's suit-clad shoulders. I wanted to roast marshmallows on his skin, breathe in heavy, woody smoke, brand my flesh with his name. I forgot about the passengers behind me. They evaporated, cooled, ceased to exist.

Jared clicked the door, slid it open, and gestured for me to go inside. I shrugged past him, my shoulders grazing his chest.

When the door clicked closed, I attacked him. I wove my fingers in his hair and smashed my mouth against his. He tasted like fine cigar smoke and dark fruit. My hands explored the expansive muscles of his shoulders. My body ached for him, lit on fire.

My skirt and underwear puddled around my ankles, and I tore at Jared's belt. His pants soon joined my skirt, and then I was flying, suspended, Jared's hands beneath my armpits, my hands on his shoulders. The backs of my thighs met the tiny metal countertop, and my head knocked into the mirror behind me. I laughed and then smiled. Jared returned the smile with mirth and hunger hanging from his lips.

He leaned forward, his hands finding my hip bones, and his mouth covered mine. Jared's tongue snaked into my mouth, and I moaned. I clasped my hands behind his neck and hooked my ankles behind his back, wanting to get as close to him as possible.

Jared wrapped his arms around me and lifted me off the counter. I could feel his heartbeat against my chest and the searing heat of his skin. With one hand, he pulled my hair back and forced our mouths apart. The crown of my head pulsed with pain, mimicking the sweet torture between my legs. I worked hard to catch my breath, staring hard at this perfect creature before me.

"Do you want this?" he asked.

"Are you kidding?" I nodded and pulled him to me.

When we bound ourselves together a few moments later, my body exploded in incendiary bursts. I felt like firecrackers were going off all around me, leaving me charred and covered in ash. My insides churned and melted, beat against my skin, reaching out to Jared like they belonged to him. I teetered on the edge of pain and pleasure, unsure of which would pull me under. I held on tight and sank my teeth into Jared's shoulder. I called out his name as I came.

And then everything went red.

XOXOX

My hands were shaking. Metal cookie cutters in various shapes were strewn around me. They would have blended in discreetly with the gray concrete of the floor if not for the blood coating them.

I was on my knees, hovering over a naked, male body, its skin a patchwork of punched-out flesh in various shapes and sticky, red blood. I began to shake from my core and my breaths came out in little, ragged pants. My stomach churned, the acid flip-flopping and boiling. I swallowed hard to keep from vomiting. I squeezed my eyes shut. There was too much red.

My head swirled and throbbed.

Where am I? And who is this? And why is there so much blood?

When my brain cooled, I forced myself to reopen my eyes. I chose to concentrate on the man's stomach, a single focal point in front of me. I figured if I could keep my sight trained on one spot, grow desensitized to the image in front of me…

My eyesight faded in and out. I wasn't sure if it was shock making the world blurry or tears that had crept into my eyes.

What have I done? Who did I hurt?

I needed to know.

I steeled myself and forced my gaze to the man's face, then let out a jagged cry. It was Jared, my muse with golden hair and marble skin, who smelled like smoke. He was so still, his eyes closed, his muscles slack, his gray lips mouthing the letter O.

I killed him, I thought, *just like I said I would.* The quaking of my body began again.

It was then that I felt the weight of something in my hand. I looked down and there was a cookie cutter in the shape of a heart clutched between my fingers. I was holding on so tight, the metal shape drew blood. Red liquid dripped off my fingers like melted ice cream and pooled next to my knees.

With a guttural cry, I hurled the cutter across the room. It clanged in the distance and then I was alone again in the silence.

I started to cry, holding my bloody hands out before me like a sadistic offering.

"I'm sorry, Jared," I whispered pitifully. "I'm so sorry."

I scooted my body closer to his face, the only part of his body that was unmarred, still perfect, save the dead skin and lifeless eyes. I leaned in close. If he were alive, he would've felt my breath on his face.

"Please come back to me," I said.

As if on cue, Jared's eyes flew open and his hands reached up to grab my face. His eyes, once golden and beautiful, now swirled with flames and threatened to suck me in.

I awoke with a start, slamming my head into the headrest and pulling against the seatbelt strapped across my belly. My breathing came hard and fast, and I could feel my pulse in my throat. My eyes darted back and forth, grasping at my surroundings. My hands gripped the armrests on either side of my body.

Armrests, I thought. *Gray plastic trays. Cheap overhead lighting.*

I closed my eyes and thought about an island, a polka dot bathing suit, and a fresh coconut with a straw. Ten seconds later, I reopened my eyes. "You're still on the plane. And that was a dream."

"Quite the dream," a voice sounded next to me.

I turned to find Jared sitting in the seat across the aisle to my left, staring straight ahead, his profile a jagged cliff. The overhead lighting was back on, so he was nicely illuminated…but he looked different.

Stone-like. Hard. *Crack.*

"I knew I was right about you," he said, turning toward me and smiling like a fox. "I'm flattered."

I frowned and thought hard, trying to make sense of everything. What had happened?

I closed my eyes and remembered the bathroom, Jared's hands exploring my body, the exquisite pain.

"I quite enjoyed that, too," Jared said.

"How do you know…?" I asked.

"Alexa, perhaps it's time for me to reintroduce myself, tell you about my job." The click of Jared's seatbelt was like a twig snapping in a deserted forest, the only sound in the cabin. In fact…I listened hard. The sound of the plane's engine had ceased. Panic gripped my belly, made it backflip.

What the…?

"I've been looking for someone like you for a long time, Alexa. Centuries, really." Jared crouched down next to me. He traced a finger across my lips. It felt like snakeskin, and I shuddered away from his touch. "Beautiful, creative, obsessed with death."

"I'm not obsessed…"

"You imagine how people are doing to die, Alexa."

How did he know that?

"My therapist…" I started.

"Your therapist is wrong," Jared said. "Your manifestations are not the byproducts of your job; they're byproducts of you, my dear." Jared leaned in close and his eyes darted up to observe my forehead. "It's a delicious brain you have."

His fingers whispered across my forearm. I pulled away and wrapped my arms around my midsection, leaving Jared's fingers aloft. He simply smiled in response.

"You see, I'm a salesman of sorts," Jared said, returning to a standing position and clapping his hands together. The sound made me jump. "Perhaps death dealer is a better title. Yes, that's more accurate." He slipped his hands in the pockets of his pants. "I'm also responsible for terror, mayhem, and panic."

I could hear my heart in my ears, and tears collected in my eyes. Trepidation twisted my stomach into knots.

Jared took a deep breath and a sorrowful frown creased his forehead. "As you can imagine, it can get quite lonely. Kill, mayhem, rinse, repeat."

He moved to the seat in front of me, put his knees on the cushion, and peered over the headrest at me, a pose that made him appear both boyish and menacing.

"And then you started showing up on my radar, which is pretty special, because there are so many people in this world, so many minds to ignore or tune in to…but yours came in loud and clear," Jared said, his features twisting with excitement. "Your thoughts make most serial killers look like amateurs. I knew you'd be my perfect match."

His eyes burned into mine. They were no longer inviting. They were cold and unfeeling. Hardened tree sap. Dead.

Three, two, one. In a flurry of movement, I reached beneath the seat for my carry-on bag. I had a pen in it, next to my journal. I could stab Jared with the pen, get away. Run up to the cockpit and sound the alarm.

But the bag was nowhere to be found.

I struggled out of my seatbelt, stood, and flung myself into the aisle, looking around for some sort of weapon to aid in my escape. As my gaze bolted around the cabin, my knees buckled, and I had to grab the seat next to me to keep from falling.

The plane was empty. No passengers, no luggage. Nothing.

Jared's laughter filled the empty space. "You should see your face," he said. "This would be so much easier if you would just let me explain."

He stepped closer. I fell into a nearby seat and pressed back into the cushion, but still his fingers found my chin. "I'm sorry, love. I'm used to taking my time," he breathed. "But I'll cut to the chase — for you."

Jared straightened and adjusted his jacket. "Everyone on this plane? Lost souls. People who were damned and promised to me. My job is to dispose of them…and then make them suffer for all of eternity. And you think your job is tough." He emitted a throaty laugh. My eyes widened. I was stuck on a plane with a raving lunatic.

Jared pulled his jacket lapels open and gestured to the breast pocket inside with one hand. "I have their souls in here. When we get home, their bodies will reconstitute, and we can decide how they die over and over and over again. Penance for their sins, you see." Jared executed a desultory hand flourish. "A plane crash is too good for most of them."

"*We?*" I didn't recognize my voice. It sounded like a weak animal.

"I'm so glad you caught on to that, Alexa," Jared said. "Yes, *we.*" He smiled, slick and oily. "You said you wanted to come with me."

Rage catapulted my voice. "To the bathroom!"

"You gave me your body."

"It wasn't a contract," I said.

"Actually, it was," Jared said. "If a woman decides to lay with the devil, her soul then belongs to him. It's one of the oldest rules in the book."

My hand flew to my mouth, and I choked on air.

"God, you're beautiful when you're terrified. Eternity will be so much better with you by my side. I just hope you never lose your fear." The thing took a step closer to me. "Scoot over, love."

I had lost all motor function. My entire body was shaking, but I was frozen, unable to even blink.

The devil sighed. "I really thought you'd take this better." He ran a hand through his hair. "But I understand. It's a big adjustment."

I squeezed my eyes shut as he hooked one arm beneath my legs and one arm behind my back. With a grunt, he lifted me from my seat. Heat radiated through his clothes. The skin of his hands was a branding iron against my skin. I heard my flesh sizzle.

The devil hoisted me over the armrest and into the next seat. He smoothed his suit and sat down next to me. "Look out the window, Alexa. We're making our descent."

Numbly, I turned my head. Outside, pine trees were ablaze all around us, the plane flying so low that fire licked the sides of the aircraft. I could hear the crackle of burning wood and smell the char of that which was once alive.

"Welcome home," the devil said, taking my hand in his. "It takes a little time, but you'll get used to the smell."

⋊⋉⋊⋉⋊⋉⋊⋉⋊⋉⋊⋉

About the Author

Tiffany Michelle Brown is a native of Phoenix, Arizona, who ran away to live near sunny San Diego beaches. She has been published by Pen and Kink Publishing, *Under the Gum Tree,* and *Shooter Literary Magazine.* When she isn't writing, Tiffany can be found drilling Aikido techniques, sipping whisky, or reading a comic book—sometimes all at once. Follow her adventures at tiffanymichellebrown.wordpress.com.

CONVERSATIONS WITH A DEAD BEAUTY QUEEN

Leigh Harlen

Alex grabbed a handful of Yvonne's shiny blond hair and pulled her face out of the bowl. Soggy globs of cereal dripped off her nose and cheeks and landed with soft plops on the table. Her eyes were wide open, and her mouth was agape. It was a humiliating way for a beauty queen to be found.

"Yup, she's dead," Janet said.

Alex pushed Yvonne back so that she was sitting up in the chair. Yvonne's head lolled to the side, and a trail of spittle meandered down the side of her chin. "Everyone will think I did it."

"Didn't you?" Janet asked.

"Well, yeah. I guess."

"You've been joking about killing Yvonne since we were six, but I never thought you would actually go through with it," Janet said, crossing her arms across her chest.

"I didn't do it on purpose!" Alex protested. "It just sort of… happened."

"Right, I just 'happen' to kill people all the time."

"I'm serious, Janet. I didn't mean to do it. You believe me, right?"

Janet sighed. "Yeah, I believe you. But I wouldn't blame you if it was on purpose." She bent over and tilted her head so she was face to lifeless face with Yvonne. "At least it was poetic. Miss Perfect Skinny Bitch dead, face first, in a bowl of slop. Now everyone will know that she actually did eat food. She would be so pissed."

"What should I do? Call the police?" Alex asked.

Janet straightened up and laughed. "Are you fucking crazy? I can see how that conversation would go. 'Gee, Officer, everyone knows

I hated Yvonne. I mean, I said it loudly and at every opportunity. I even admit that I poisoned her. But it was an accident, honest!'"

Alex pulled out a chair and sat down next to Yvonne. The table jostled the body, and Yvonne's head landed back in the bowl, sending milk and gelatinous bits of cereal flying. A cold mushy glob smacked into Alex's cheek. She grimaced, wiped it off with her hand, and smeared it on the table. "So what should I do?"

Janet sat down across from her. "Well, we could go on a spree. Knock off a few vapid Barbie dolls and then make a run for Mexico."

"Well, that's one possibility. But I was sort of hoping for good ideas," Alex said.

Janet grinned. "I guess we should hide her somewhere unless you want to spend the next fifteen to twenty making license plates."

"As Yvonne would be quick to point out, orange is not my color."

Janet looked at her watch and stood up. "I have an appointment. It would look suspicious if I skip it. We'll figure something out as soon as I get back. Make sure no one sees her."

"Thanks, I'll try to remember to not let anyone see the dead body in the kitchen." Alex rolled her eyes.

Janet left, and Alex was alone. She stood up and pulled Yvonne's face back out of the cereal and slid the bowl away. She let her head fall back down with a thud. Alex sat back down.

Yvonne's cheek was pressed against the table. A clump of blond hair, matted and sticky with milk, clung to her forehead, and her glassy blue eyes seemed to stare right at Alex.

"Well, Yvonne. Here we are," Alex said to the corpse. "This might be the first time we've ever had a conversation where you didn't call me a lazy fat ass or a useless moocher."

Yvonne sat there, silent and dead.

"In fact, this might be the first conversation we've ever had where you let me say anything at all. You really were a mean, spiteful bitch." Alex was enjoying this. After ten years of misery, it was cathartic. "Now I have to figure out what to do with you. So, you've managed to fuck me over, yet again. I'm sure you're thrilled."

"I'm dead, mooch," Yvonne said. She raised her head off the table with stiff, jerking movements until she was sitting straight up. "Forgive me if I'm not exactly sad that you're finding the situation inconvenient."

Alex jumped out of her chair, and it clattered to the ground. "Jesus fucking Christ. You're dead!"

"And you're as perceptive and eloquent as ever, Lexie. Yes. I'm dead. You killed me. What do you have to say for yourself, cousin?" The corners of Yvonne's mouth turned up in a smile, and she raised one eyebrow. Alex always hated that condescending, haughty look of hers.

"I didn't do it on purpose," Alex insisted.

Yvonne laughed. "A liar and a murderer. Your parents would be so proud."

"It's true. I mean, it's true that it was an accident." Alex righted the fallen chair and sat back down.

Yvonne pursed her lips and nodded. "Of course. It was an accident. I'm sure you just tripped and dropped poison in my coffee. Which one of us is a mean, spiteful bitch, again?" Yvonne laughed.

"I…I…didn't…I mean—"

"'I…I…didn't' what? Want me dead? Of course you did. You hated me. God, I can't believe I was murdered by someone who wears cargo pants," Yvonne said.

"No, I didn't. I mean, yeah, I hated you. But I didn't want you dead."

The doorbell rang.

"Oooh, that will be Brad. He was really excited that I finally agreed to go out with him. He's going to be so disappointed." Yvonne stuck out her lower lip in a mocking pout.

"I'll go get rid of him," Alex said, standing up.

Yvonne giggled. "Oh dear, I hope he doesn't insist on seeing me. I am not looking my best today."

It wasn't Brad. A pudgy man with "Jeremy" stitched on his olive uniform stood on the porch.

"Hi. Are you Mrs. Bellerose?" he asked, sounding disinterested.

"No. I'm her niece." Alex tried to sound calm but every inch of her body was flushed and sweating.

"Okay. Well, I got a call that you had a leak in the kitchen sink. I'm here to fix it," he said.

Alex's heart started pounding, and her mouth went dry. She considered telling him to reschedule, but how could she explain to her aunt why she sent him away? "Hold on just one minute." She shut the door in his startled face.

"Oh! I forgot to tell you. Daddy called a plumber to fix that leak in the sink." Yvonne gave her a mean smile.

"Shut up, Yvonne." Alex glared at her.

Yvonne smiled. "What ever will you do now, Lexie?"

"How many times do I have to say it? Don't call me 'Lexie.'"

Alex scooted Yvonne's chair out, and her corpse fell sideways onto the floor with a loud thud.

"Smooth," Yvonne mocked.

"Is that the best you can come up with, Yvonne? You really must be dead." Alex bent over and grabbed her by the ankles. She dragged her body across the white and blue tile floor, down the hallway, and into Yvonne's bedroom.

Even Yvonne's bedroom made Alex want to vomit; it was lemon yellow and pale pink, and everything seemed to be covered in lace and ruffles. She dropped the body on the floor.

The side of Yvonne's mouth was pressed against the carpet, making her words mush together. "That all took a suspicious amount of time. I wonder what he thinks you're doing." Yvonne's muffled laughter followed Alex as she ran down the hall.

Alex opened the front door. Jeremy was tapping a clipboard and looking angry. She gestured for him to come inside. "Sorry about that. The kitchen is through there." She pointed.

He nodded and followed her. He looked at the mess of milk and cereal on the table and wrinkled his nose.

The doorbell rang again. Alex groaned.

"Hey, is there a bathroom in here?" Jeremy asked.

"Yeah, it's down the hall on the right," Alex said as she turned to go answer the door.

She looked through the peep hole and saw a tall, blond man with a square jaw. He was wearing a too-tight black T-shirt with the sleeves cut off to display his well-muscled arms and poorly drawn tribal tattoos.

Alex opened the door. "I'm guessing you're Brad."

He looked her up and down, and his expression suggested that he was not impressed with what he saw. "I'm, uh, here to see Yvonne."

"Right. She's sick. Sorry." She started to close the door, but he put his foot in the way.

"You must be her cousin."

"And you must be an asshole."

He crossed his arms across his chest, making his biceps bulge, and glared down at her.

Alex sighed. "Yes, I'm Yvonne's cousin. Good guess. Bye."

"Yvonne warned me about you. She said you were jealous of her and liked to cause trouble. I'd like to hear it from her."

Alex clenched her jaw. "Yes, well, I can see how she might think I was jealous and wanted some dim-witted, steroid-filled suitors of my very own. But she is, in fact, sick."

"Why wouldn't she call?" he asked.

"How many times do I have to say that she's sick? Maybe the incredible has happened, and she's so delirious she forgot how to operate the phone."

He stepped toward her, and the overwhelming smell of cheap cologne and hair gel made Alex cough.

"I want to see her."

"She doesn't want anyone to see her. She's been vomiting all morning. Her hair's a mess, and she's not wearing makeup. Girls like her don't let guys like you see them looking like that."

For a moment, Alex thought she won. At the mention of vomit, he looked far less sure of himself. But then he gave her a determined stare. "I'm not leaving until I see her."

"Oh, Christ. Hold on. Wait right here. I'll wake her up and warn her that you're coming."

Alex ran through the kitchen. When she stepped into the hall, she saw the plumber standing at Yvonne's door with his hand the doorknob.

"Don't go in there," Alex shrieked.

He looked startled and stepped back. "I was looking for the bathroom."

"I did say on the right, didn't I? Does that look like the right?"

Jeremy's face flushed. "I'm sorry. My mistake."

Alex considered apologizing but then she remembered Brad standing in the living room. She opened the bathroom door. "Right here."

Jeremy nodded and walked down the hallway. Alex waited at Yvonne's door for him to go inside. He looked back at her with a perplexed expression, but, at last, he went in and closed the door.

She slipped into Yvonne's bedroom.

"It's a bad idea to let him see me. Brad won't believe that I'm just sleeping," Yvonne said.

"Shut up. He's a moron. He'll believe it. Just keep your damn mouth shut for a change."

"You can't," Yvonne said.

"I can't what?"

"You can't let him in. I will not be seen like this. I have cereal in my hair. My makeup is all smudged."

Alex shook her head. "You're seriously worried about your makeup right now?"

"What? Just because I'm dead, I don't get to have standards? I'm not you."

"He's not going to see you. We actually agree on something for once." Alex said, covering Yvonne's body with a fluffy pink comforter.

"Will you at least brush my hair?"

"No."

Yvonne gave a dramatic sigh. "Fine. You'd probably just make it worse anyway. I mean my god, have you ever even bothered to run a comb through your hair? Or are you afraid you'd disturb the ferrets who have clearly begun nesting in that mess?"

"I'm sorry I choose to spend my time on things other than my hair."

"You should have spent some of it on plucking your eyebrows."

"Do us both of a favor, and shut your mouth. Or Brad is going to see that glob of cereal on your nose and the dried drool on your chin."

Alex went back to retrieve Brad. He was standing in the doorway looking angry.

"She's sleeping, so keep your mouth shut and follow me."

She led Brad to Yvonne's bedroom. All that was visible was a lump under the blankets and a cascade of blond hair.

Alex whispered, "See, she's sleeping. Satisfied?"

Brad glared at her, but he nodded.

"Now get the hell out so she can rest," she said.

Alex followed Brad back to the living room. Janet was standing in the entryway, and Brad stomped past her and out of the house without a word. She locked the door behind him.

She turned to Janet. "Thank God, you're finally here."

"Who the hell was that? You let someone inside?"

"He didn't leave me much choice. And that's Brad. He was here to see Yvonne. There's a plumber in the kitchen, too." Alex gave a nervous laugh.

"Shit. Why not get a keg and invite the whole neighborhood?" Janet whispered.

"Like I said, I didn't have a choice."

Janet shook her head. "Christ. Where's Yvonne?"

"In her bedroom."

"So, did you think of a place to get rid of corpse Barbie?" Janet asked.

Alex shook her head.

"We could take her out on your Uncle's boat and drop her in the lake. But we'd need something heavy to put her in so she doesn't bob to the surface," Janet said.

"There's a metal storage box in the shed. I think she'd fit."

Janet looked thoughtful, and then she nodded. "That sounds perfect. Is your van big enough?"

Alex nodded. "Yeah, if we put the back seats down."

The plumber stepped around the corner. "Were you talking to me?"

"What? No," Alex said.

The plumber looked confused. Then he shrugged. "The sink is fixed. I left the bill on the table."

"Thanks," Alex said. She opened the door, and the plumber left. She breathed a sigh of relief.

"Let's pull the van up to the shed. I'm guessing it's a heavy box. And then we can take Yvonne out the back."

Alex nodded. They hopped into the van and drove over the well-manicured lawn. Alex unlatched the shed door. The box was still there, covered in dirt and cobwebs. Her uncle had bought it to store some of his more valuable equipment, but the lock had been busted years ago. Now there was nothing but a tarp and a lot of rope inside. She pulled everything out and threw it on the floor.

Together, she and Janet dragged the box to the back of the van. They paused, and Alex wiped sweat from her brow.

"On three," Janet said. "One, two, three." They got the edge of the box up into the van and pushed it the rest of the way in.

Janet waited by the van while Alex went inside to get Yvonne's body.

"Seriously? This is your brilliant plan? I'm going to sleep wit' da fishes?" Yvonne said with an exaggerated wise guy accent.

"That's the idea," Alex said. She grabbed Yvonne's wrists and dragged her off the bed. She landed on the floor with a thud. Alex dragged her through the house and out the backdoor.

The large box left no room in the back for a corpse. She crammed Yvonne's body into the passenger seat. She slammed the door shut before the corpse could tumble back out.

Alex wiped her sweating palms on her jeans. "Do you think people will really believe that she's sleeping?"

Janet shook her head. "No, but they'll believe she's wasted."

Alex climbed into the driver's seat. She pushed Yvonne back with one hand and pulled the seat belt across her body with the other. When she heard the buckle click, she started the engine.

Janet knocked on the window. "Where am I supposed to sit?"

Alex looked back, the box took up the entire back of the van. She cranked the window down. "There's no room."

Janet craned her neck through the window. "Maybe I can fit on the floor."

Alex shook her head. "You should stay here."

"Why? I can fit. Besides, I want to watch." Janet said.

Alex shook her head. "You've already risked enough because of my fuck-up. Besides, if we get pulled over, I might be able to pass Yvonne off as drunk. But I don't want to be doing something else illegal."

Janet frowned. "If you're sure."

"I'm sure." Alex waved goodbye and backed the van up through the yard. Yvonne's head thumped against the window when the van rode over the curb and onto the street.

Yvonne laughed. "You didn't think to put me in the box first? I can't believe you managed to kill me. You're so dumb, I can almost believe it really was an accident."

"Shut up."

"Oooh, brilliant comeback," Yvonne taunted.

"Seriously, Yvonne. Shut the hell up."

"Or what? You'll kill me?"

Alex pulled the van up to the empty lot in front of the dock. Ice still clung to the edges of the small lake. Her uncle had put the boat in a week ago because he wanted to make room for a new truck in the garage.

Alex grabbed the box and pulled it out of the van. It landed with a loud clang. She gritted her teeth against the sound of the metal screeching across the pavement as she dragged it. When she reached the dock, she shoved the box over the edge, and it landed in the bottom of the boat.

She returned to the van and opened the passenger side door. She unlatched the seatbelt, and the body fell out in a heap on the ground. She grabbed Yvonne's wrists and pulled her. The skin on Yvonne's heels and calves scraped on the rough surface.

"Lexie, Lexie. Don't you watch television? Some handsome man with glasses and great hair will find these bits of me you're leaving everywhere."

Alex grunted. "No. They won't. No one is going to look for you, Yvonne. I'll tell everyone that you got knocked up and ran off with some guy. They'll believe me."

"Now that would be just scandalous. No would believe I was such a slut," Yvonne said with a dramatic gasp.

"Newsflash, Yvonne. People already believe that. People don't actually like you. Being hot is not the same thing as being liked."

"Maybe. But it's better than being a despised slob, don't you think? Remember when you used to get dumped at my house all summer? You sat in my room alone, playing with your invisible friend. You weren't even a likable five year old."

Alex rolled the body over the edge of the boat, and Yvonne landed with her legs sprawled on the seat and her head on the floor.

Alex untied the boat and jumped over Yvonne's body. She dug under the driver's seat for the key. She started the motor and pulled away from the dock.

She stopped the boat in the center of the lake. She dragged and shoved Yvonne's body into the box. Alex paused for a moment, the body was in a tangled heap with legs sticking out so she couldn't close the lid. She pulled and arranged Yvonne's crumpled limbs in an attempt to get the corpse to lay flat. But Yvonne was too tall and her body was too stiff. She wasn't going to fit.

"Shit."

Yvonne rolled her milky eyes. "You really are a moron. You didn't even bother to the measure the box? You're going to be known as the worst murderer in history."

"I am not a murderer. It was an accident," Alex said.

"Sure it was, Lexie. You're dumping my body in a lake because it was an accident. So what's your next brilliant plan?"

"It *was* an accident," Alex said. She sat down and thought. "If you won't fit, I'll have to make you fit."

"You're some kind of genius, aren't you?"

Alex yanked and pulled Yvonne back out. She opened up a crate where her uncle kept emergency supplies. She tossed energy bars, water bottles, and bandages around the boat until she found a small ax. She gripped the damp wooden handle with her cold fingers and took a deep breath.

"You can't be serious. First you kill me, now you're going to mutilate me? I'm not actually sure which the greater crime is."

"I don't have a choice.

"Lexie, we both know that's a lie. But what can I expect from someone with parents like yours. So what's it going to be? My shapely legs or my beautiful face? I'd prefer you go with my legs. Either one would be a tragedy really. My legs looked damn good in a mini skirt, but who would I be without my beautiful face?"

Alex clenched her jaw. "One head will be easier than two legs."

"Oh come on. Admit it. You think cutting off my head sounds more fun. It's so much more personal, don't you think?"

Alex brushed Yvonne's golden hair aside so she had a clear view of her pale skin. She raised the ax and brought it down with all her strength on Yvonne's neck. It bit into skin and muscle and stuck. Alex jerked it free and struck again and again. She heard bone crunch, and her own voice screaming into the frigid wind. When Yvonne's head came free, the ax bit into the wood floor. Blood leaked out of the stump, but it wasn't the spurting mess Alex expected.

She stood up and looked around, the lake was still empty. She set the head behind her.

She grabbed the headless corpse under the arms and wrestled it back into the box. It fit this time. She took a step back, and her ass bumped into Yvonne's head. It rolled off the end of the boat, landed with a splash, and sank below the surface.

Yvonne's hysterical laughter burbled up through the water.

Alex hooked her feet under one of the back seats and stuck her head in the water. It was so cold that it sucked the breath from her body. She thought she saw something in the murky water, and she reached for it, but it was just a shadow. She pulled her head out, and her wet hair soaked through her jacket.

"Fuck! Fuck! Fuck," Alex screamed, but it was useless. The head was gone.

Alex looked down at Yvonne's headless body one last time and then slammed the lid shut with a loud clang. She braced her feet and shoved the box off the end of the boat. It slid into the water, bubbled, and disappeared from sight.

She started the motor and returned to shore. A part of her expected to see flashing lights and police waiting for her at the dock, but it was still empty. She tied up the boat and ran to her van. Away from the lake and driving down the road, she breathed a sigh of relief.

When she arrived at the house, the driveway was empty. She didn't have to worry about her aunt and uncle yet. She went inside, leaving wet footprints on the floor.

She entered the kitchen and screamed.

Yvonne's head was lying inside the cereal bowl, staring up at her with an amused smirk. Her long, blond hair was matted with mud, and her bluish skin was covered with ice.

"That was really sloppy," Yvonne said. "I mean, my God, Lexie, what do you think daddy will think that is on the bottom of his boat, cranberry juice? Honestly, I'm ashamed to have been killed by someone so inept."

"For the last time, I didn't mean to kill you," Alex shouted.

"Yes, you keep saying that. So do tell, how did you manage to poison me 'by accident'?"

Alex crumpled into the chair across from Yvonne's head.

"I'm sorry, there must be some seaweed in my ear. What did you say?" said Yvonne's head.

Alex shook her head. "I just wanted to make you sick. I didn't want to kill you."

"Ah, yes. You just thought you'd give me a stomach ache. You must admit, that sounds extremely unlikely." Yvonne's head raised its eyebrow.

"As much as I hate to agree with her, she has a point, you know," Janet said, standing behind Yvonne.

Alex screamed. "Where did you come from?"

Janet shrugged. "I never left. Look, Alex, you did the world a damn favor by killing Yvonne. Why not just own it? There's nothing to feel bad about, and no one here is going to tell on you."

Alex swallowed. "Because I didn't mean it. I was angry. I wasn't thinking clearly. I just wanted to make her throw up."

Yvonne chuckled. "What did you have to be so angry about?"

Alex gripped the edge of the table, and her knuckles turned white. "You. I'm so sick and tired of you. Every day it was, 'Now Lexie, be grateful that we agreed to take you in while your momma's in jail.' And 'Lexie, why don't you wear something that doesn't look like it came from the spinster cat lady collection.' So yes, I was angry."

"I don't think it's fair to be angry with me just because I provide you with some constructive criticism. I mean, I would want to know if I was loser with ugly clothes."

The doorbell rang. Alex screamed through gritted teeth. She yanked the door open so hard that the knob dented the wall.

A police officer stood on her front porch looking surprised. Alex felt as though a vice had clamped down on her chest. She glanced back at the table. Janet raised an eyebrow, and Yvonne made a kissy face.

"I'm sorry to disturb you, Miss," the officer said.

Alex tried to keep her voice from trembling. "Can I help you?"

"Yes, one of your neighbors reported some items stolen from their garage this afternoon. Someone from your house reported similar thefts a few months back. I'd like to ask you a few questions." He pulled a pen and a notepad out of his pocket.

Alex nodded. "Yeah, go ahead."

"Could we step inside?"

Her body trembled, and she shook her head.

The officer took a small step backward and narrowed his eyes. "Are you alright, Miss?"

"I'm fine. The place is just a mess right now."

"I promise, I don't mind. It's freezing out here. And you look like you just got out of the shower."

Alex glanced at the kitchen. Yvonne was hidden by the wall. "Okay. Come in," Alex said and stepped back from the door.

"Thanks, my name is James," he said. He shut the door behind him and wiped his feet on the rug.

"Hi. I'm Alex. I'm the Belleroses' niece." She did her best to block his view of the kitchen and Yvonne's head.

James squinted at her in the dim light. "You're shaking. Are you all right?"

Alex tried to answer, but she couldn't think of any explanation. As the silence grew, the officer tensed and started scanning the house.

He put a hand on her shoulder and started to lead her into the kitchen. "Mind if we talk in here? It's awful dark in the living room."

Alex choked on a scream that turned into a yelp. But she couldn't think of a way to stop him.

"Alex, why don't you have a seat?" He pointed at the table. Alex shook her head and stared at Yvonne. The officer continued to talk, but his voice sounded far away.

"Say, he's pretty cute," Yvonne said.

"Christ, even dead you're a skank." Janet rolled her eyes.

"There's no getting out of this now. I was right, worst murderer in history. But on the up side, my funeral is going to be amazing. I can't wait to see how many people come. I bet they all cry. Go on, Alex. Tell him how it was just an accident that you killed me."

Janet walked over and draped her arm around Alex's shoulder. "Don't listen to the bimbo. So, it wasn't exactly an accident. The world is better off with one less superficial bitch making everything even shittier for the rest of us."

"I didn't mean to," Alex whispered. The officer went silent and stared at her.

Yvonne winked. "Of course. All that research, all that planning. All by accident. I definitely believe you. Honestly, I have no idea how more people don't accidentally poison one another." Yvonne started laughing, making her head rock back and forth until it tipped the bowl, rolled off the table, and landed at Alex's feet. Yvonne blinked her ice-coated eyelashes and stared up at her.

"Miss? What didn't you mean to do?" the officer asked.

"What you did was a public service. You have nothing to feel bad about," Janet whispered in her ear.

"Tell him you're a pathetic loser, and you killed me because I wasn't nice enough to you."

Alex shrieked and grabbed the officer by the shoulders. "They're right. I did mean to do it. I killed her and she fucking deserved it."

)O(O)O(O)O(O)O(O)O(O)O(

About the Author

Leigh Harlen is a speculative fiction writer whose work often has a dark bent. Their writing has been published in *Aurealis, Dark Moon Digest,* and *Turn to Ash.* When not writing, they can typically be found wandering Seattle petting strangers' dogs. Follow Harlen on Twitter @leighharlen for updates on future publications and pictures of bats.

HORROR AT
HALLOWS CROSS

R J Murray

On a cold day in early October, two young women arrived at the village of Hallows Cross. They had become tired of the gypsy lifestyle, of the constant travelling, and decided to settle somewhere quaint and peaceful, just the two of them.

Gretchen was somewhat familiar with the area, having spent some of her youth residing in the wilderness nearby before her kin and their colorful wagons were moved on by the council. She remembered the beauty and allure of that part of the country and decided to take Morven to witness it for herself. The village had seemed perfectly suited to their needs, and so they explored the area looking for an appropriate abode.

As the women reached the outskirts of the village, they happened upon a strangely endearing church building, which immediately piqued their interest, and so they decided to probe further.

An imposing iron cross, heavily rusted, mounted the entrance wall of the church, desolate and solitary, upon a wild moor. Silent in its surrender, creeping ivy possessed the black walls, the iron door, the spire. The church yard was overgrown with grass and weeds, while moss-covered gravestones punctuated the landscape like a morbid rockery.

Previously when the church has been in use, there had been a number of thatched houses nearby and even a small shop, but now the long-abandoned area stood excluded from the community, a newer church having been built within the heart of the village.

Both taken with the dark Gothic beauty of the old church building, and as unconventional as the women's tastes were, they decided immediately to take up residence. Despite its dark, cold, echoing interior, they were quite enamored with the prospect of such a unique dwelling. The church had long been disowned by the state, and therefore no authoritative opposition was posed.

They acquired furniture from the market, as well as linen, crockery, and an old stove. Candle sconces were mounted along the dark walls, which illuminated the stained-glass images of saints and angels etched upon the windows. An old iron bed was placed in the upper chamber, at the top of the spiral staircase, where a fractured painting of Jesus on the cross gazed down from the high ceiling.

Half a century before, lightning had struck through the roof of the building, and while some obvious repairs had been carried out, there remained an unusually large and misplaced-looking glass skylight. Gretchen and Morven were impressed by the feature and were soon welcoming by day, the sun — its conjuring rays dancing in beams down the spiral stairs — and by night, the moon — its imposing sphere lighting up the upper chamber with a secret glow.

As could be expected within such a small community, mindless gossip and rumors had circulated about the two women. Some condemned their relationship; some accused them of sinful living, of witchcraft. The latter accusation was not completely without truth as both women were spiritually and magically inclined. As pagans, they worshipped the earth, grew herbs in the old church yard, and regularly practiced healing and meditation rituals.

Still, the women were not imposed upon by the community, and it wasn't long before they settled into their new home. Morven, having previously trained as a teacher, took up a post at the village school. Gretchen continued her knitting and needlework, creating patchwork blankets and tapestries that she sold at the weekly market.

The women continued in their routine and began to feel quite content in their new home and situation, that is until the day Gretchen became ill. Prior to that day, she was not fully without complaint, mentioning vague headaches in the evening and an apparent problem with her ears (high-pitched sounds which Morven had no register of). But it was when Morven returned home from the school one day to find Gretchen laying across the bed, weeping and convulsing, she knew her ailments were worse than first imagined. In a panic, Morven called the village doctor, who examined Gretchen quickly, proclaiming her to have a virus and advising it would soon pass. He offered to write a prescription for some pills but seemed quite on edge and keen to leave, as if his presence in the women's home was somehow a detriment to his reputation or beliefs. Morven sensed his unease, which, in turn, made her angry, and she rashly asked him to leave. She had no tolerance for small-town prejudices and so stubbornly resolved to take care of Gretchen by her own means.

From the oil and herb cabinet they had set up in the lower floor, she gathered drops of clove oil, peppermint, ginger root, and arnica, mixing them together in a clay bowl. She sat by the iron bedside, a cold compress on Gretchen's head, administering the remedy in drops to her tongue and singing gypsy melodies, the bedchamber lit only by a waning moon. Within a few hours, Gretchen's temperature decreased, and both women slept peacefully into the next morning.

The next day, Gretchen returned to working on her tapestries and Morven to the school. In the evenings when Morven came home, they would sit at the oak table where Gretchen served dinner: fresh boiled vegetables from the yard and meat bought at market that day. The candles would be lit, and the heat from the stove warmed the hall. For the first time, the women felt a strange conventional air to their situation they never had previously, because their lives prior had been dictated by quite the opposite. Gypsies they had always been and, as such, lived a life of unpredictable days and long winding roads, without roots or responsibility. They had felt almost rebellious at leaving that life and becoming what they had never known. Now the initial novelty had faded away, and it all began to feel ordinary and mundane. While they both had these thoughts, neither expressed any doubts to each other. Their mutual love and feelings remained unchanged, and they took comfort in each other's affection, tenderness, and continued attraction.

Two days passed by where, as usual, the women saw each other only in the evening. Gretchen had appeared to be more withdrawn than usual, saying little and turning in to bed early. Morven, also tired, attributed this to Gretchen's recent virus and thought nothing of it. However, the next morning over breakfast, Gretchen blurted out quite unexpectedly that she wanted to have a child. Her manner was abrupt and unusually erratic. Morven was so surprised, she felt unable to respond. They had discussed children at length in the past and their decision not to have any, and nothing since had been said or done to indicate such a change of heart. In fact, they had both been quite resolute on the matter. Morven has always known she was challenged reproductively and probably couldn't conceive even if she had wanted to, whereas Gretchen had openly professed to having no maternal urges, despite the love and care she had felt toward her younger siblings and cousins.

Morven, although confused, agreed to discuss the issue and understand Gretchen's needs. But despite her attempts at a reasonable heart to heart, Gretchen seemed to fall under a sickly fever again. She refused to talk, complaining of various troubles and head pain. During the night, she rarely slept, suffering from night tremors that caused her to awake screaming uncontrollably into the darkness.

Understandably, Morven was distraught. She barely recognized Gretchen as she was behaving, and felt increasingly helpless at how to deal with the situation. She lay awake worrying until the first rays of sun beamed into the church, casting specks of light, reflecting down from Jesus. Then, for the first time in days, Gretchen rose from bed, bright eyed and jovial and with her arms lovingly draped over Morven. She explained her desire to have a child had been sudden, but she genuinely considered it her calling and their new fate together. And then to Morven's amazement, she professed with a frenzied energy, a knowing in how to conceive naturally by the earth, by the sun, and through the spirit. After her burst of vigor, she suddenly turned pale and fell onto the old armchair, staring into a void. As anxious as she now was, Morven stood silently and reached for her hand. She knew something was off, that some hinge in Gretchen's mind had been switched, changed. That she wasn't well. Morven's heart sank yet she nodded in pretentious agreement, and they both sunk into an embrace.

The next morning as Morven walked to school, she couldn't think of anything else but Gretchen. What had got into her? She speculated she could still be feverish. Maybe she had a serious illness or the onset of some mental ailment. Or perhaps she was feeling uneasy in the new situation, homesick for her family, her siblings. Or maybe Morven didn't know her as well as she thought she did.

Back at the church, Gretchen was full of energy and purpose. She gathered and prepared her herbs, tools, and utensils in order to conduct the first ceremonial ritual. She had clarity, focus. She knew what she had to do.

Acorns were scattered in the dark corners of the building. Bergamot and Lady's Mantle was added to water, then poured into a bathtub of rose petals, thorns, and morning dew. After the soak, she wrapped a black velvet cloak over her body and ascended up the spiral steps.

Under the skylight, she scattered salt and ivy leaves in a circle around her feet and chanted the words:

Fertilonias Corronios
Fertilonias Corronios
Fertilonias Corronios

She threw off her robe and lay spread-eagled under the eyes of the archangels, pouring drops of jasmine, rose, and lavender and massaging them onto her stomach, pelvis, and hips.

The next day, she drank rose hip tea at first rise of sun, and in the evening, brewed a potent concoction of sage and elderberry, which she sipped slowly in the bedchamber, under the full moon.

Despite Morven's anxiety, she couldn't help feeling moved by Gretchen's new lease on life. She'd never seen her so full of passion and purpose. That night when Morven returned home, she was met by Gretchen in a delicate lace negligee, who then led her to the bathtub, lit by soft candles and filled with pink petals. She undressed Morven, and the two women made sensuous love as the ballads of fairy tales played softly from the gramophone.

The next morning as Morven walked to School, she felt invigorated by the night before, but her rational mind couldn't deny that something was wrong. Yet, the more she pondered having a child, the more the idea brought unusual feelings of tenderness and excitement. Maybe they could have a family, but despite Gretchen's strange aspirations and ideas of conception, a man would most certainly have to be involved. Wouldn't he? She was more concerned over the fact their rational communication had seemingly broke down completely. She felt she couldn't possibly mock or contradict Gretchen's vision of faith, which she seemed so decidedly fixed on. Yet she must, mustn't she?

Morven continued with these thoughts during the day and was losing concentration in class. It must have been noticed, as the following day, Mrs. Forrester, the school superintendent, asked to talk with her in the office. Being as vague as she could, Morven apologized and explained she had been distracted recently with some personal issues at home. Stern as Mrs. Forrester was, she accepted this, and Morven returned to class.

Later in the day, while Morven was filing some text books in the library, she could overhear Mrs. Forrester talking on the telephone. As she just made out the words "the old church," she stopped with curiosity, placing her ear close to the door.

"Of course, not many would wish an association to that building; I wouldn't go within earshot of..."

A door seemed to slam, and Morven jolted back into the library until the footsteps echoed away toward the outside door. She wondered what Mrs. Forrester could have been referring to and what possibly could have occurred at the old church. She knew lightning had struck it but nothing more. As she walked home past the village, her mind was flaring up with curiosity, and she decided to do some research on her day off. There were very limited resources within the village and as she had no friends within the community, she concluded she would have to visit the nearby town, Degway, to look at historical records. Most likely, there would turn out to be nothing of interest, but still, she looked forward to the change of scenery and routine.

So it followed that Morven left early the following Thursday and made her way into Degway by coach. Gretchen had declined joining her, professing a need to finish a tapestry piece she was working on. Morven was relieved, looking forward to some time alone.

The records library was larger than she had imagined, and Morven was enthralled by the sheer content of information on offer. Such was the efficiency of the filing and display systems, she was able to find with ease the local news and historical pieces available. After not much time, she located a newspaper article dated half a century ago, which as she scanned, caused a deep feeling of unease.

Reports of a recent weather incident involving Hallows Cross Church have been challenged by meteorological experts who were left perplexed by the occurrence. After a thorough investigation, it seems a suspected lightning storm did not take place, and officials have announced a further investigation to explore possible causes for the strange disaster.

Following the incident, Rev. John Kilshannon, priest of the parish, was reported to have been left distraught, adopting a somewhat irrational and aggressive state and refusing to depart from the building in order for urgent repairs to be carried out. Many locals reported various peculiar and erratic actions before his final "descent into madness." The events were finalized by Rev.. Kilshannon tragically taking his own life, plunging from the upper skylight of the church building and onto a stone wall, his neck instantly breaking and his skull shattering.

Morven felt a shiver down her spine with the realization that this was the same building where she went to sleep every night. It almost felt tainted, cursed.

There was another listing which had name-checked the building, but when she found the extract, it was from an unusual occult textbook where nearly all of the inscription was written in what looked to be Egyptian hieroglyphics, with swarms of unintelligible symbols. There was also a map and diagram that appeared to be a star chart of constellations, but she disregarded it, unable to make any sense of it.

When she arrived back to the village from the coach, she was eager to tell Gretchen all about their home's morbid history, but when she walked through the door, she wasn't prepared for the scene before her. Gretchen was kneeled on a stone step, halfway up the staircase beneath the skylight, and chanting the most inhuman noises. She had her hands clasped together as if in prayer, and her body was rocking to and fro. Morven looked on in disbelief, and as she stepped on the stairs, her shoe became stuck. There was some sort of black sticky substance dripping on the stone. Morven screeched out in disgust, pulling her foot free. Gretchen stopped and looked at Morven with an innocent smile, an odd glint in her eye.

"What are you doing? Are you okay?" Morven asked.

"Oh, a fertility ritual. I'm finished now."

"It sounds like you were in pain! What an earth is that black stuff?"

"What? Oh. I was experimenting with some mixtures. It's nothing." Gretchen looked strange, distracted, glancing around the room as if she'd lost something.

"Well, listen! I must tell you all about this place. You won't believe..." But before she could finish, Gretchen stopped her.

"I'm tired," she said, yawning. "I'll hear about it another time."

Gretchen stepped up the winding staircase toward the bedchamber.

But it's only seven o'clock, thought Morven. She slumped down at the table, her head in her hands. As she thought about the grizzly findings at the library and the increasingly strange behavior of Gretchen, a sickly feeling began to grow in the pit of her stomach.

Morven spent the rest of the evening alone, sipping a bottle of wine and reading one of her historical fiction novels. She eventually fell asleep fully clothed, slumped on a cushion over the old wooden pew, while the wind whistled secrets through slender window panes.

She awoke the next morning with a chronic headache but, unlike Gretchen's, she could clearly identify the cause. As she got up from the pew, she noticed a tarot deck had fallen off the wooden shelf, and the cards were scattered over the floor, a single card upturned. The nine of swords. Morven gasped.

A bad omen.

She put the cards back and mopped up the black liquid, which had now congealed on the tiled floor and railings of the stairs. When she had finished cleaning, she prepared a pot of tea and carried it up the staircase to Gretchen, only to almost drop the tray in shock at the sight in the chamber. Gretchen lay sprawled out on the bed on cotton sheets that were now stained black, congealed, and dripping with the same substance on the steps from the night before.

"What the hell? *Gretch?* This black liquid is everywhere! What's going on?"

Gretchen turned around and gave her a vacant glance.

"I told you. It's a fertility exercise I'm trying." She lazily rose from the mattress, gathering the soiled sheets like it was a regular occurrence.

"Well, you can clean it up this time," spat Morgan. She dropped the tray of tea on the chest and stormed down the staircase, grabbed her coat, and left.

She had a deep, unsettling feeling as she walked toward the village. She always did after a disagreement, but this felt worse, like she had no control over anything. She felt she was losing Gretchen, losing the connection between them. Maybe she had to be more attentive and understanding, if Gretchen really was sick, she considered. Maybe it was herself who was being selfish and intolerant.

When Morven got home, many hours later, she was so exhausted that she went straight to the upper chamber where she was met with two strange-looking black cradles sitting by the bed. Slender, with Gothic spires, they rocked to and fro and were filled inside by delicate white lace blankets freshly knitted by Gretchen.

Gretchen, who was sat by the window, responded to Morven's questioning expression with a gleeful grin, blurting out that she had seen the doctor and that she was pregnant with not one but two babies! Twins! After the news, she had found the beautiful antique cradles at an estate sale on the outskirts of the village, and the proprietor had kindly delivered them to the church.

Morven was stunned. Gretchen sensed her disbelief and reassured her it was quite true and that her fertility work had been a success. Morven tried to show affection and delight, but felt too uneasy with the whole strange situation. She couldn't quite believe it, yet restrained herself from expressing doubt and instead allowed Gretchen to chatter incessantly about her hopes and plans and feelings about the babies.

The next day in the village, Morven dropped in to see the doctor who confirmed in a disapproving tone that Gretchen was indeed pregnant and that she would need special medical attention due to the fact it was her first pregnancy and a multiple birth. He confirmed some future appointments and suggested she attend as many as possible. Morven responded rather embarrassingly that she would indeed and hastily departed the office.

Walking over the cobbled path to the school, she felt a rush of pain to her temples. She couldn't process what was taking place. It was literally a miracle. *But how?*

It was a question that remained unanswered, despite all of Morven's confusion and attempted communication with Gretchen. She decided to ignore her better judgement and find a way to accept and welcome the prospect of these potential children into her life. Gretchen had become her true self again and bloomed marvelously with the trimesters that followed. She had become consistently warm and affectionate and seemed happier than she had ever been. Morven soon felt quite content with the situation, and as they planned ahead as a future family, everything fell into place.

The hopeful spring arrived, and when she wasn't at school, Morven began drafting the novel she had always talked about but never found time to begin. Gretchen spent afternoons knitting tiny baby booties and hats and gathering daffodils from the garden to brighten the church inside. When summer arrived, she tidied up the church yard, placing an old rocker on the patio, where she stitched beautiful woolen shawls in the sunlight. She gathered vegetables from the patch and prepared seasonal soups to enjoy in the evenings that were now bright and cheerfully illuminated by saints in the stained-glass windows.

The pregnancy passed by without a single worry, and as the leaves began turning ginger, and the frost transformed the moss into white crackling, Gretchen had almost reached full term.

Then, on the night of old Hallows Eve, at almost midnight, one girl and one boy were born inside a candle-lit church, into the arms of two delighted mothers. The twins had bright green eyes, full heads of jet black hair, and were perfectly formed.

The babies never cried yet were extremely healthy, immediately eating and sleeping well. However, following the birth, Gretchen herself had become poorly. The headaches and tiredness had started again, and when the babies were sleeping, she constantly complained of high buzzing noises. Often, she awoke in cold sweats, calling out as if in danger. Consequently, it was left to Morven to take responsibility and attend to both her and the babies. She took temporary leave from the school and prayed to herself it would indeed be temporary. Despite her keen intentions, she struggled to feel genuine motherly love for the babies but resolved to be patient, and to throw herself into their care and attention, if only for Gretchen. She dreaded the thought of Gretchen's health further declining and tried not to imagine the worst.

Early one morning just after dawn, Morven was changing the babies when she noticed on both of their tailbones a faint mark of an identical and unusual nature. She thought it odd she had never noticed this before, and there seemed something familiar about the particular shape of the markings, something that seemed to cause a vague recollection or a memory she couldn't quite fathom. She pondered for a moment but then dismissed the thought, knowing it was not uncommon to be born with this type of birthmark. After she changed and fed the children, she placed them back in the adjoining cradles next to Gretchen. The lace covers enveloped their bodies like perfect gift wrap, and just as they always did, the children fell fast asleep.

An hour later, as Morven was walking home with shopping from the market, she felt a violent shudder down her spine, making her stop suddenly. As she stood in the wilderness, surrounded by tall grass and ancient trees, she looked up to the sky that had suddenly turned a deadly black. Immediately there appeared a sudden spark of light forking down in a zig-zag, illuminating the landscape, like a flicker of fire, then darkness again. This was followed by a horrifying howl that traveled through the wind and lingered, like the sound of a captured soul. With her heart beating like a drum, she began running over the hill toward the church. The rain had started to pelt down, and the wet mud began to congeal over her boots, splashing over her skirt and bag. She kept on until she could see the church, then raced madly toward it.

Through the iron door she went, dropping her bags and racing up the spiral stairs. As she ascended, she could feel the rain and wind battering at her from the ceiling. She looked up to see the skylight had been shattered, a million shards scattered in pieces on the floor below. Across the back wall of the chamber, dripping in black slimy liquid, had been scrawled a large symbol. The very same symbol as marked on the twins. Rapid thoughts swam through Morven's head. *The occult book in the records library…the constellation chart…Why didn't I realize? Why didn't we leave? I should've insisted. I knew about the building; I knew it was cursed!*

A chair lay upturned under the shattered skylight, which she maniacally lifted and stepped onto. Peering down into the drenched, morbid yard, she screamed in horrifying realization as she spotted Gretchen's body, her white nightdress now stained red, impaled upon the iron gate.

She turned back into the chamber, convulsing with the kind of dark despair she never thought possible.

She gazed at the rocking Gothic cradles. Empty.

Black slime oozed from the spires, the sides, the iron base.

And as Morven's desperate screams escaped from the open roof and caressed the heights of unknown peaks, they continued to rock. To and fro, to and fro.

)()()()()()()()()()()(

About the Author

RJ Murray is a writer and musician inspired by all things dark, Gothic, and offbeat. She has published several short stories and is currently working on a novel. She lives in Scotland with her family and cat Willow. Poetry, news and stories can be found on her blog: https://rebeccajmurray.wordpress.com/

ALWAYS CONFINED

Adrian Ludens

Unaware that skeletons would soon burst from his closet, Johan Weber sat gazing out the grimy nursing home window. His brain had wandered far, far away from his present confinement. He soared over fields, drinking in the sights of verdant endless green like a flower drinks rain. Then, from somewhere, someone spoke his name.

"Grandpa Johan."

The voice sounded close at hand. It pulled him back to the present, back to reality, though he resisted at first.

Like a dog returning from an adventure, knowing the confines of a cramped kennel waited, his mind resigned itself to the inevitable. He became aware of the ever-present odor of human waste, bathroom disinfectant, and burnt pot roast.

Johan looked up from his bed sheets into the smiling, expectant faces of strangers. He scoured his memory, summoned up the face of his only grandson, Michael, and matched it to the man of about forty who stood before him now. With him was a small girl. Most of Johan's great-grandchildren were girls — that much he remembered without much deliberation. The gears in his brain slipped but engaged again after only a moment. The little blond girl had her father's eyes and a bubbly, precocious personality. Her sister, a shy brunette several years older, was named Rhonda. That meant this child's name was...

"Vonnie!" Johan said. "Well, aren't you the prettiest little girl I ever did see!"

Yvonne Weber beamed up at her great-grandfather. "Yes, Great-Grampy."

Johan chuckled at her childlike honesty; as far as she knew, he was simply stating the truth. He put out his hand.

"Gimme five."

The little girl smacked his upturned palm and giggled when he winced and carried on as if she'd broken it.

"My land! You put some hot pepper into that five, didn't you?" Johan said.

"Yes, Great-Grampy." Yvonne said and skipped to the window. Perhaps she, too, craved escape into wide-open places.

"We brought you something, Grandpa," Michael said. "An early birthday present."

Why? Johan thought. *Don't you think I'll last long enough to see my next birthday?* Aloud he said, "Oh?"

Michael produced a black gadget Johan thought might be a journal. Instead, his grandson unfolded the contraption. Johan squinted. "What is it?"

"It's a laptop," Michael said. "Now don't worry; there's nothing to it. Here, look."

His grandson started explaining how to send email but Johan paid little attention, only nodding when it seemed appropriate.

Then Michael opened another window on the computer. "Now, this," he said with a grin, "I know you'll like!"

He slid his fingertip on a rectangular pad at the bottom of the keyboard, below the letters. Somehow this allowed him to control the computer.

"We got you a subscription to a digital radio service." Michael told him the name of the company. To Johan, it sounded like the name of a Russian satellite from during the Cold War.

"They say music helps improve people's moods and can even help with memory. I preset some music channels for you, Grandpa Johan," Michael said. "To listen to classical, all you need to do is click here." His grandson paused and turned his head to ensure the older man was watching.

"Okay," Johan said, noncommittally.

"For country, click here. For jazz, here. See?"

"Sure."

"To control the volume, you click here." Something flashed on the corner of the screen and then disappeared. "Got it?"

Johan didn't know what to say. "Well, this is a thoughtful gift. Thank you, Michael. I hope it didn't set you back too much."

"Oh, no worries!" Michael said. "I figure I can get it back later when you...uh...get bored with it. But keep it for as long as you want."

Johan caught his grandson's slip but let it pass. He was right, after all. Any day could be his last, and he wouldn't use foolish pride or fear of what came next as an excuse to deny the facts.

"Thanks again. Mighty nice of you." Johan's rheumy eyes swept the room until he found his great-granddaughter practicing awkward pirouettes in the corner near the window. "And thank *you*, Vonnie!"

"You're welcome, Great-Grampy!" the girl chirped, all smiles, blond braids, and boundless energy.

Michael looked at him expectantly. "Are you comfortable sending emails? I added a bunch of family addresses to the address book."

Johan wondered where this book was located but decided against asking. He didn't want to look foolish. "If I get stuck, I'll get one of the nurses to help."

"Any questions about the digital radio?"

Johan had to admit he was curious. "How does it work, exactly?"

"Well, I don't know *exactly* how it works, but you never have to worry about weather interference, static, or commercials because it all comes from a satellite."

Ah-ha! Johan thought, scowling. "A Russian satellite? The name sounded Russian."

Michael only laughed. "No, it's just a regular American satellite. It's harmless. The signal is beamed from 22,000 miles above earth to your radio and about two million others just like it."

Johan narrowed his eyes, but said nothing. *People today were too trusting, too soft,* he thought. They didn't understand what previous generations had experienced, had sacrificed.

"C'mon, Vonnie, time to go," Michael said.

They said their good-byes and left Johan alone in his sterile room, surrounded by dirty-white walls, ensconced in silence. He thought about his fellow residents, most packed two to a room. Johan considered Michael and Vonnie, encapsulated in their car, headed home. He even imagined the satellite, 22,000 miles above earth, yet confined to its orbit.

He lay back, closed his eyes, and dozed.

When he awoke, the sun had nestled on the horizon. Johan knew dinner would soon be served. He felt well enough to make his way down to the dining room, but didn't feel particularly social so opted to remain in his room a while longer.

His eyes strayed to the computer. How had Michael gotten the music to play? It had something to do with the blank pad on the keyboard. Johan reached out and touched the panel and saw the small arrow on the screen move in tandem with his finger.

When the music burst from the speaker, the sounds of a swinging big band yanked him back into the past — to the darkest chapter of his life.

Darkness and shades of gray.

Whispers. Everything in whispers. Always.

"Johan."

"What, my love?"

"Frau Klein says the people who supply the food coupons have been arrested."

"Did they betray our location? Are we in danger?"

"I don't think so. I hope not. Say a prayer that we can remain here in safety. But, Johan?"

"Yes, my love?"

"All we have now are the black market ration books."

"Perhaps we can give them to Frau Klein. She can bring us food."

"Perhaps."

A sound woke him. His heart pounded with fear.

Darkness in abundance. His voice a whisper.

"Leah, what's wrong, my love?"

"I am not well."

"You are sick?"

"Yes. I'm sorry."

"Shhh. You mustn't cough."

"How can I stop?"

"You must."

"I know. But my lungs threaten to betray us."

"I shall ask Frau Klein if she can help us."

"How?"

"Broth for your stomach. Beer, if she can spare it, for your cough."

Life in hiding and seclusion felt like prison. Johan wondered about the camps, if the rumors were true. Perhaps they hid needlessly.

"I miss touching you."

"I miss your touch."

"Maybe I can..."

"No, Johan, stay there. I don't want you to fall ill."

"I want to hold you."

"I know what you want. You can have it when I am well."

"But, Leah..."

"When I am well."

Leah lay on her dirty cot mattress and coughed discretely. Johan slouched in a corner of the attic where he knew no boards would squeak. The angled room was dark and stifling. Husband and wife were alone with their thoughts. Johan did not know what Leah thought about. He did not ask.

Below them, Frau Klein had turned up a radio. Swing music played. The music soothed Johan, so he focused on it. A big band played a familiar number, but Johan took notice of something odd about the vocalist's enunciation of the lyrics.

Gradually, and with great care, he stretched out and pressed his ear to the rough attic floor.

"This is the story of Winston the Whiner; he knows we'll bomb him out of his bunker."

Johan gasped, drew attic dust into his lungs, and choked as he tried to stifle his cough.

"Johan?"

"It's all right, my love."

Despite his coughing fit, they whispered out of habit.

He knew those weren't the right words. Had he imagined them?

The song ended and another began. The melody was familiar. The vocalist — the same fellow as before, Johan thought — sang a familiar refrain at first but the second time around the lyrics changed.

"There will be vultures flying over the white cliffs of Dover, feasting on Allies who should have known better."

Enraged, horrified, Johan scrambled across the attic floor.

"What is it? What's wrong?"

"Don't worry, my love. I mean to get to the bottom of this right now."

He found the trap door and descended in a mad scramble. They rarely dared enter the ground floor of Frau Klein's home, especially without their protector's invitation, but anger guided his movements.

He strode into the room to find her alone and dancing. She froze when she saw him, her eyes widening. "Johan! You shouldn't be down here."

He bared his teeth, the closest he could come to a smile. "I apologize for intruding, Frau Klein, but that music is intolerable."

She smoothed her hair, breathing fast. "Is it too loud? That would be bad." A look of genuine distress came to her face. "I don't want the Gestapo knocking on my door saying they heard degenerate music coming from my home."

"*You* don't want the Gestapo knocking on your door?" Johan asked, incredulous. "Imagine how we feel! And the radio program would be the last of your concerns; what about harboring Jews?"

"You don't understand," Frau Klein said. "It's complicated."

"The words in the songs are awful, despicable!" Johan trembled with rage. "How can you harbor us, keep us safe, yet listen to such hate?"

"My husband, Herr Klein, he joined the military. He took a lot of pride in his country."

"I know this, but..."

"He died. Killed on the Russian front. I just found out from a..." her face crumpled, tears flowed. "A telegram! They didn't even send someone!" Frau Klein sank into a chair and erupted into sobs that shook her entire body.

Johan didn't know what to do. Words seemed cheap, gestures meaningless. He stood awkwardly until she regained some measure of composure.

"My husband is dead and gone, taken from me while defending a cause I don't believe in. I am here, left with nothing."

"I am sorry for your loss, truly I am." Johan paused, grasping for the right words. "But the lyrics to the songs are ugly and hateful. They don't match the person Leah and I know you to be."

"I am rebelling." Frau Klein said. She gave him a sorrowful look with puffy, bloodshot eyes.

"Rebelling against what?"

"The Nazis."

"But the words..."

"I don't listen to the words."

Johan felt his eyes widen in disbelief. His anger rekindled and his mouth grew dry. "It's propaganda! How are you able to listen to such a broadcast? Swing and big band have been labeled *negermusik*, and are banned here now."

"Yes, but the music thrives underground here in Hamburg. Haven't you heard about the swing kids?" She didn't give him time to answer. "But I don't dare go out and attend those dances. It would only draw attention to me, and then, perhaps, to you."

Johan couldn't argue with her logic but the question remained: "Frau Klein, the man sang about the dead bodies of the British. The broadcast is outrageous."

"It's meant to be. The band plays the songs faithfully but with new lyrics. The idea is to crush the spirit of the Allies, though it probably only serves to incite them to further action. The broadcasts can only be heard on short wave and some medium-range radio. My husband built this set before he enlisted. It was his hobby."

"So you listen to Nazi big band propaganda broadcasts as a form of rebellion?" Johan furrowed his brow, trying to understand.

"My husband is gone, and I am alone. And why? What will all this killing, this death, accomplish?" she asked. "The music soothes my aching heart, takes me away from my sorrow, if only for a few moments at a time." She sat up straighter. "And listening to pirate broadcasts of something that *der fuhrer* has banned gives me a small satisfaction."

Johan wrestled with her words and his own feelings on the matter.

"If I don't listen, I will go mad with grief," Frau Klein said. She gave him a long look.

Johan shifted uncomfortably under her scrutiny.

"Do you know how long is has been since I've felt the touch of a man, Johan?"

"I'd better go back to the attic," he stammered. His face burned, and he felt an instant stirring below his waist. "Leah will be worried — and she's sick, as you know."

He turned and clambered up the ladder into suffocating darkness, leaving Frau Klein to her storm of emotions.

"Leah."

He crawled to where she lay. "Leah!"

She started, said something unintelligible, and looked at him with bleary, uncomprehending eyes. She licked her lips and tried again. "Johan?" Her voice was raw from illness and muddled from sleep. "What is it?"

"Will you hold me?"

"Yes." She held out one arm, and he nestled against her. A clammy sheen of sweat covered her skin, but he did his best to ignore it. He was so hard he ached. He reached out and stroked her gaunt face. When his hand moved down to cup her breast, Leah's eyes opened.

"You know I can't. We must wait. When I am well."

"I only..."

"When I am well."

Johan closed his mouth to seal off any further protests. His need proved to be a stubborn thing, however, and his body would not permit itself to relax. He held her for a time, and when her breathing slowed, he crawled back to his customary corner.

His hand strayed beneath his trousers. A burst of big band brass jarred him from his intentions. The music now came even louder.

The band charged through a swinging number Johan recognized and despite his desire to shut the music out, he laid immobile, ears straining to hear what the man sang in place of the original words. Johan did not have to wait long.

"Sorry Jew boys, it's not the Chattanooga choo-choo, let the SS decide which camp we're going to send you."

Enraged, Johan scuttled across the attic floor and threw open the trap door. As he descended, his fury mounted. He ran into the room where he'd confronted Frau Klein before. The tinny music grated his eardrums. She stood next to the short wave radio and turned it down as soon as he entered.

Johan skidded to a halt. Her appearance rendered him speechless.

Frau Klein wore high heels, white stockings, a garter belt, and nothing else. She'd unpinned her luxurious brown hair, and it cascaded over one shoulder like a waterfall of dark chocolate.

"I knew you'd come," she said, her voice husky with desire yet also trembling with sorrow.

Guided by his own physical needs, Johan fell into her arms. They kissed roughly, then she yanked down his trousers, and they made frantic love on the first piece of furniture they fell onto.

Johan crawled back up the ladder scratched, sweating, and satisfied.

In the attic, an almost palpable silence reigned.

Guilt asserted itself and guided him to his wife. How much of what had just transpired had been audible? He crawled up to her cot mattress and took her hand.

Her skin felt cool. Thinking her fever had finally broken, he kissed her forehead only to find it cool and dry.

"Leah?"

She didn't respond.

"Leah."

He shook her arm. Pinched her cheek.

"Leah!"

Johan clasped his hands around hers, sick at heart and weeping. What had been her last words to him? A cacophony of random thoughts created so much white noise in his brain that he couldn't remember. What had he last said to her? When had they last kissed or held hands? When had they last walked together under the night sky or laughed over a joke one of them had made? He couldn't remember.

He couldn't remember, but he would try.

Johan spent the remainder of the night sitting up beside her remains, reminiscing.

When the muted songs of morning birds began, Johan kissed Leah's forehead again and mentally asked her forgiveness for leaving her there.

Then he exited their attic refuge with more silence and stealth than he ever had mustered.

By the cobwebby gray light of dawn, he made his way into the room where the short wave radio sat on a table.

He stooped and peered at the equipment, searching for the knob that would turn the music back on. The semi-darkness, combined with his own unfamiliarity with the short wave set, combined to stifle his efforts.

When he turned away in disgust, an elongated white shape lying on the floor caught his attention. He stooped to retrieve the object and then returned to the table. Johan swept his arm out and knocked the radio to the floor. He kicked it for good measure. Then he hurried to the wall beside the room's only entrance.

When Frau Klein, wearing a nightgown, rushed in to investigate the sounds, Johan stepped up from behind her and dropped the stocking he'd retrieved from the floor around her neck. She fought him, but he used both hands to hold the ends of the stocking. He funneled the ends through his cupped left hand and wound the fabric around his right, cutting off her air...

Johan came back to himself, back to the present, and found his gnarled hands wrapped around the laptop's black power cord. The cord was wound around a woman's throat.

In horror, he dropped the cord, and the nurse gagged and yanked it from her neck. She scrabbled across the tile floor of his room and hauled herself to her feet. The nurse — her name was Cassidy, he remembered — clutched at her throat. Her face was a red as a blood moon.

"You crazy old bastard," she rasped. "You could have killed me! You damn near did!" She erupted into a series of dry coughs and tears streamed down her cheeks.

"I'm sorry! I got confused..." He took a step toward her, arms outstretched.

"Stay away from me!" She warded him off. "I'm calling the cops." Cassidy turned on her heel and fled from the room.

He, too, had fled, he reflected, seventy years ago. He left two dead women — one he loved, one he resented — behind in a nondescript house in Hamburg. He'd raced through the streets like a lunatic, instinct kicking in as he fled apprehension, yet mentally he'd resigned himself to his fate.

The Gestapo caught up with him on the outskirts of the city and took him into "protective" custody. He even signed forms stating that he feared for his life, which, in a way, had been the truth, but he knew he'd receive no protection from these glowering men. They put him on a train, confined in a cattle car with more people than he cared to count. Some prisoners remained cautiously optimistic, while others wailed and lamented their fates. Johan found himself wavering between the two stances. After two days, he arrived at a place that reeked of death.

Two months later, the Allies had liberated his camp, and Johan fled again, this time to America, where he toiled for meager wages and slept in a room as small as the Hamburg attic. He remembered the eventual office job, the string of claustrophobic apartments, meeting someone and marrying — the wedding had been conducted in a tiny chapel. His entire life, he'd never managed to rediscover the sense of freedom he'd once known, as if he'd left that gift behind with his dead wife.

He felt constantly confined. Always fleeing, always confined. He envied the radio waves shooting through space.

He rifled through the bottles on the medication cart the nurse had left behind. He'd nearly taken another innocent life. Johan swallowed hard, trembling. Never again. He squinted at each label in turn, searching for one that would help him escape. His hands seized on a bottle he knew could do the job — if he took enough of its contents.

He shook a pile of pills into his palm. Today, he reflected, he would at last find the permanent freedom his spirit so desperately craved.

⋊⋉⋊⋉⋊⋉⋊⋉⋊⋉⋊⋉

About the Author

Adrian Ludens is a radio announcer living in the Black Hills of South Dakota. His latest story collection, *Ant Farm Necropolis,* was recently published by A Murder of Storytellers, LLC. Adrian enjoys watching hockey, swimming, reading and writing horror fiction, listening to all types of music, and exploring abandoned buildings. Other recent anthology appearances include the *HWA Poetry Showcase IV* and *Zippered Flesh 3*. Visit Adrian for updates, a cover gallery, free stories, and more at www.adrianludens.com.

THE TRAIL

Don Cox

T erry's house was only a mile away, but walking a mile in the dark was different; a mile in the dark was a long mile, the longest.

Terry was dreading the walk as he left his friend's house. He pulled Max's door shut, barricading himself from the brightness and warmth of Max's rowdy but happy home and exposing himself to the indifferent silver light of a full moon and the frigid wind of a late November night. He popped the collar of his thin jacket and stuffed his gloveless hands into its pockets. The wind bit painfully at his ears and nose and watered his eyes.

Bending into the wind, Terry crossed Max's manicured lawn, hopped his picket fence, bounded across the empty street, and reluctantly entered the dense woods beyond it.

Separating Terry and Max's suburban streets was a long, narrow tract of wilderness where tall pine trees fought scrubby bushes and rocky outcroppings for growing space. A beaten trail littered with pine needles wove through the trees to a crumbling bridge spanning a swift, narrow stream that cut through the woods like a blue vein. He and Max used it daily, running from one house to the other. It was a needed shortcut for twelve-year-old boys who were too young to drive. Terry knew it well; he loved it during the day and hated it at night.

Tonight, the trail looked no wider than a shoestring, unfamiliar and strange. The woods stretched ahead of him, filled with grasping shadows and eerie sounds, and he had the feeling the bushes and trees were concealing things, dangerous things.

Right now, he wanted to be playing Max's new game, destroying video game zombies, instead of imagining them lurching toward him in the dark. But it was late, and he had to get home.

"Knock it off," he told himself. "You're too old to be scared of the dark."

He ducked his head against the wind and walked, his feet crunching frozen needles. The moonlight helped until thick black clouds swept in and seamlessly blanketed the moon, blocking its pale light, throwing the woods into a deep darkness, making Terry feel blind. Squinting his eyes, he tried to see where he was going. Childhood fears tightened their grip on him.

"Panther piss," Terry said. "There's nothing out there."

A loud warbling howl coming from behind him answered this declaration. He spun like a Marine executing an about face, searching the dark in blind horror. The howl faded, stopped, and then started again. Terry stood paralyzed, sweat breaking out on his cold forehead. He had never heard anything like it. He had heard coyotes and even wolves before. This was neither; this sounded human.

The second howl faded like the first. Terry stared hopelessly into the dark. Something lumbered through the trees and then crashed into a bramble of bushes. The bushes rustled, dead leaves crunched, and branches snapped as loud as ladyfingers. He looked harder, straining to see in the inky darkness, his heart beating like a jackhammer.

Bending down, he reached out and grabbed the first thing his hand touched, and he stood up holding a heavy pine branch.

He sucked in a deep breath as the bushes shook louder. It sounded like an animal, a large animal, was trapped in them, thrashing around, trying to escape. The cold bare branches clattered against each other like dry, fleshless fingers, causing an awful noise. Terry didn't remember to exhale until it stopped. Nothing moved. He watched the darkness.

Were those eyes he saw? *Quit it*, he thought. But he had seen eyes, high off the ground, not an animal's. The eyes moved closer. He heard it breathing. Terry gripped his branch like a baseball bat. His fists squeezed until its cold bark dug into his palms. The woods went quiet, and Terry waited.

A growl, like a large dog's, broke the silence, floating to Terry's ears like soft music. A twig snapped on the trail. His mind raced with indecision: run, fight, scream? Whatever it was, it didn't give him time to make up his mind; heavy feet pounded as it ran at him. Branches snapped and rocks scattered as it charged. Terry screamed and swung, twisting his hips for power like in Little League.

He swung as the clouds broke apart, the moon came out, and everything slowed to a crawl.

The moonlight lit up the world, and Terry saw Max's chubby laughing face. At the same time, Max saw Terry's stick headed for his left ear. Max's face changed from amusement to shock.

Terry planted his feet, trying to stop, and his feet slipped out from under him. Terry watched helplessly as his makeshift club whistled around. Terry excelled at baseball, and he knew he was going to kill his friend. But Terry's panicky aim was high, barely, and the branch merely brushed Max's long, unruly hair.

Terry's swing jerked him around like a big leaguer striking out, and the branch collided with a tree behind him. The hit stung his hands, sending vibrations up his arms, and snapped the branch into pieces. He dropped what was left of the branch and looked down at Max. Unbelievably, he was laughing, lying on his back looking at Terry; the look of fear and bewilderment on Terry's face made him laugh harder.

"Whoo," Max cheered, "that was a close one."

Terry didn't laugh. He was too mad. Mad enough to be tempted to grab another branch. *No one would know,* he thought, *I'll say, "No, Mrs. Adams, I don't know what happened to Max."* Instead of reaching for a club, he reached out his hand and helped Max off the ground.

"Ah thanks," Max said.

"Whatever," Terry said. Then slugged Max in the arm and yelled, "You nearly gave me a heart attack, jerk wad."

The punch hurt Max enough to shut him up, and he just stood there rubbing his arm.

"Sorry, man," Max said, but before Terry could decide if he meant it, Max started laughing again, "But it was too funny."

Terry acted like he was going to punch him again, and Max flinched, throwing his arms up in defense; Terry felt a little better.

"What are you doing out here?" Terry asked.

"Cleared it with our parents; no school tomorrow, so I'm staying over," he said. Like a peace offering, he pulled off a red backpack from his pudgy shoulders and opened it. Inside was his game console and *Apocalyptic Zombie Destruction*. "And of course, I brought this along."

Terry tried to look unimpressed, but a crooked grin spread across his face. Max laughed, victorious.

"All right," Terry said, "but you're still a jerk."

"Let's go," Max said.

Terry led the way along the curvy trail. Their breath puffed out in white clouds, which were swept away in the wind. Walking with Max, Terry's fear loosened its grip a little.

"You gotta admit, I got a realistic howl," Max said, each word coming between deep breaths.

"I don't have to admit anything," Terry said. "I knew it was you the whole time."

"Yeah, how?" Max asked.

"Because I'd know you anywhere," Terry said and walked faster down the trail.

Max laughed and jogged to catch up. Then he took a deep breath, tilted his head back, eyes staring at the moon, and howled.

Max's howl rose in the air like a mournful siren. It sounded real enough to raise tiny goose bumps on Terry's arms, something Terry would never admit.

"Knock it off," Terry said.

Max howled until it faded out like the end of a bad song; he drew in an exaggerated breath and laughed. As they walked deeper into the woods, Max let out more howls. Terry walked faster. Max caught up and howled again, but choked on it when a guttural howl answered back.

It sounded nothing like the make-believe howl of Terry's chubby friend. Max's seemed like the whispering cry of an asthmatic baby compared to it. Terry's arms didn't break out in goose bumps, this time his whole body flared up in big white knots, tightening his skin like a drum. The howl swelled in the night, spreading through the trees and drifting off on the wind. And as if the howler commanded the skies, the clouds covered the moon again, encasing them once more in darkness.

"What was—" Max began but the howl came again, cutting him off.

This time louder and closer. Fear didn't grip Terry this time; it crushed him in an iron fist. Both boys felt panic shoot through them like poison, and they ran. They tore off into the woods, abandoning the trail, running away from that horrible sound.

Expecting to die at the hands of an unnamable horror that they were sure was nothing but teeth and claws, they ran into a jumbled wall of thorn bushes and screamed. The sharp thorns tore their clothes and drew shallow, bloody scratches on their skin. Realizing what they were in, they fought their way out and searched wildly to see if they were being chased. Nothing moved in the dark; they held their breath and listened. Unnatural quiet descended on the woods.

The silence was heavy, joining with the night, becoming tangible; Terry could feel it. *Make a joke, Max*, he thought, *Make a joke so we can laugh, and we'll be safe*. If Max broke the silence, they would be okay; they could go home. But Max said nothing. Terry pleaded silently for him to speak, or laugh, or anything, but it wasn't Max who broke the silence.

The loudest howl yet invaded the woods like a tsunami of sound. The howl was saturated with emotions Terry's child-mind didn't fully understand: rage, lust, misery, and insanity. It was an evil sound, rabid and hungry. It was the howl of a legion of demons, escapees from the bowels of hell, singing in chorus. It was the sound of something of unimaginable size: big, bigger, biggest.

The howl cut off, with a crash of colliding canines, followed by thunderous barks and deadly growls. A tree crashed to the ground, and the beast roared.

"Run," Terry whispered, and it came for them.

It wasn't like a nightmare when the monsters move as silent as shadows; its charge was a din of violence. It ripped a path of destruction like a tornado, making no attempt to weave its way around obstructions. Trees toppled, bushes were shredded, and rocks were crushed as it hurtled toward them.

Terry grabbed Max's hand and dragged him away from the approaching horror. The boys ran blindly through the woods again, bouncing off trees like pinballs. When they tripped, they used their momentum and rolled right back up to their feet. Both boys were soon covered in dust and pine needles. Terry was faster than Max; he half pulled, half dragged him along. The noise of their mad dash was lost in the disturbance of their pursuer. They ran as fast as they could, but it was faster.

The wind pushed the clouds past the moon, and its pale, precious light enabled them to see well enough to run faster and dart around obstacles. They squeezed through a dense growth of trees, and Terry saw the silver light of the moon reflecting off of the stream.

If he could make it past the stream, he could make it home. Terry thought, *it's only a quarter mile from there.* The bridge was nowhere in sight, but he didn't care; he would deal with the cold water. *If it was January, I'd just run across the ice,* Terry thought.

Both boys were panting like runners at the end of a marathon, their energy sapped by their panic. Max tripped on a protruding rock and would have gone down, but Terry held him up, using all his strength keeping them both from going down.

"I can't," Max moaned.

"Try," Terry said and pulled harder, every second losing ground.

They cringed every time it assaulted their ears with monstrous roars and deep, slobbery growls. The ground shook as it trampled through the woods. Tears streamed down Terry's face as he ran. The trees ended twenty yards away from the water, and they burst into a smooth meadow covered in dead grass.

"Come on," Terry yelled.

Terry sprinted all out, but Max was like an anchor hanging onto him. Terry jerked Max's arm, trying to make him move faster, but he only hopped once and almost fell down.

Terry threw frightened glances behind him and saw what was tearing through the trees. It was a hulking beast running on two enormous legs, with wolf-like feet, tearing into the ground of the meadow, leaving deep gouges. Its massive body was covered in dirty, matted fur. It raised its long muzzle, pointing its lupine nose toward the moon and howled, then snarled and opened a wide mouth, dripping with the blood from whatever poor creature had last crossed its path. Terry marveled at its sharp teeth, like ivory railroad spikes. Its bellowing roar sent thick drops of frothy spittle flying off its muzzle, and Terry saw them glisten in the moonlight. And he could smell it. With each desperate breath he took, his nose was saturated with a smell of moldy, corrupted earth, spoiled meat, and the coppery odor of blood. Its burning red eyes met Terry's. He saw death in those demon's eyes as it launched itself across the meadow.

Terry knew they wouldn't make it to the stream, much less to home. He was going to die in the dark, in the cold. But he ran anyway. He was twelve years old, and he wanted his mama. He ran for home; he ran to survive. Ten feet away from the stream, Terry let go of Max's arm and kicked out with his leg at the same time.

Max went down hard, face planting into the frozen mud on the stream's bank with a loud smack. Not looking back, Terry jumped as far as he could into the cold water. He made it three quarters of the way across before plunging in. The shock of the cold water hitting his sweaty skin nearly killed him. Water reached his neck before his tippy-toes touched the muddy bottom. The waves of freezing water crashed over his head and ran down the back of his neck and into his open mouth, stinging like needles. His body convulsed with shivers, and his teeth chattered noisily. Fighting the stream's current, he swam to the other side.

"Terry," Max said, hurt and confused, with blood running from his cut cheeks and tears from his eyes.

Terry climbed out on the other side and turned around. Max was pushing himself up and trying to run at the same time. As Max's right foot splashed into the water, Terry watched the monster swell in size like an attacking lion as it hurled itself at Max. Its gruesome form slammed into Max like a thunder clap. The two bodies flew into air. Long fingers with long sharp claws tore into Max as they hit the middle of the stream. Boy and beast disappeared beneath the surface, buried in an avalanche of water.

Terry backed away, horrified, as blood rose to the surface of the water. His body shivered from terror and cold. He coughed out icy water that burned his lungs and breathed in great gasps as he tried to catch his breath. A terrible cramp tore at his side, and he fell to his knees.

After an eternity of a couple seconds, they breached the water like two submarines. The wolf held the kicking and screaming kid in its giant claws, shredding his clothes and skin like wet tissue paper. Opening its mouth, it buried its muzzle into the soft flesh between the neck and shoulder. Its jaws snapped shut like a hunter's trap, and its teeth ripped away sinewy flesh and muscle. Blood sprayed out in a fountain, black in the moonlight. Max let out a desperate screech, and it howled in triumph. Terry thought those mingled sounds would drive him mad. He turned from the nightmare and ran through the trees for home.

Terry didn't look back. Narrowing his senses, he saw only what was right in front of him, blocking out everything else. He did not feel the cold or the tree branches he ran into. He blocked out all thoughts. He blocked out what he had seen, heard, and smelled. He blocked out what he had done.

His tunnel vision ended when he burst out of the trees, his sneakered feet landing on hard blacktop, his pale face cast in orange light from the neighborhood houses. He turned right and saw the welcoming light of his own front porch and ran to it. He choked with sobs of horror, guilt, and worst of all, relief. Unable to stop running, he hit the front door like a hammer. His frozen hands groped but couldn't turn the doorknob. He cried, expecting to die on his own doorstep. Soon the monster would slaughter him and drag him back into the woods, back to Max. And part of him knew he deserved it. He looked back, and his mind conjured the wolf coming for him, dripping with blood and water. He tried again, and the doorknob mercifully turned, and he let out an ecstatic sob as he fell into the warmth of home and slammed the door behind him.

His worried mother was running down the hall, as he was locking the deadbolt, asking where he had been, why was he so wet, and where was Max. The questions died on her lips when she saw the terror on his face. He told her the first thing that came to him.

"Max fell into the stream when we were crossing the bridge, and he disappeared under the water. I tried to find him, but I couldn't." He blurted it out through gasps and sobs, and then he ran, leaving her in shock. Fleeing up the stairs to his room, he slammed his door, stripped off his wet clothes, and huddled in the dark, wrapped in thick blankets, listening to the howling wind.

Downstairs, his mom made phone calls.

That night and for the next few days, they searched for Max. Then they searched for his body, far down stream from where Terry had left him. Terry had reluctantly been taken back into the woods (during the day, only during the day) to show them where Max had fallen in. He knew his story and never deviated from it. It was a terrible accident.

The search ended when the first snowstorm hit.

Eventually, Terry went back to school. He didn't speak to anyone, and no one spoke to him, but they all stared. They stared at him as if they knew the truth.

That night, he woke from a nightmare, just like every night since Max died.

Winter was singing tonight. He listened to the storm outside. His window faced the woods, but it was covered, blocked out with heavy curtains. Lying in the dark, he tried not to scream. The nightmare lost its hold on him as he sucked in deep breath after deep breath, but the images became clearer instead of evaporating like a normal dream. The wind rocked the house, and snow pelted his window. Lying down to go back to sleep, he heard a familiar howl.

"It's just the wind," he spoke out loud but with no conviction.

It was the same howl that chased him in his dreams. The howl he had been waiting for, never doubting its escape from his nightmares. It came closer to his house, growling, stamping its heavy, padded feet, and barking hellish barks. Terry moved to his window on disobedient legs. He knew what was out there, and he didn't want to see it right below his window now.

Terry pulled back his curtains and looked down into the storm. The full moon's light shone through a break in the clouds, making the falling snow glow. It was there, of course, looking up at him. Even through the storm, he saw it clearly: big and grotesque in its mutated abnormality. Its hairy body shook with fury as it paced back and forth, leaving giant paw prints in the fresh snow. Vicious snarls and horrid growls drifted up to him on the wind. It was hungry, and Terry knew he was the only thing to satisfy it. It looked at Terry through the window and roared. Terry stepped back. It howled again. This wasn't the monster that chased him a month ago. He knew, not because of its childlike howl; he knew because he would know Max anywhere.

XOXOXOXOXOXOXOXOX

About the Author

Don Cox is a retired United States Marine who has traveled the world. A fan of the outdoors, sports, and reading, he lives in Ramah, New Mexico, with his wife and five kids.

My Dearest Lenore

Timothy A. Wiseman

My Dearest Lenore,

I know what I am about to do will hurt you, but I think it is best for everyone. There is no way that I can prevent the problems this will cause for you, but I hope they are not too severe. I want you to at least understand why I am doing this, and to understand that you must know things about me that I have never told you before.

By the time you were born, I was a writer. Whether you could call me successful might be debatable, but I earned enough from my writing to support us, even though you often complained about how well I might be supporting you when you were a teenager. My road to becoming a writer was somewhat convoluted, but I had always wanted to be a writer of some kind.

My earliest memories were not of my parents or my dog, but of grand fantastic universes I held in my mind. The first things I remember were things I had imagined. My next earliest memory was of telling my mother of some of these things and her scolding me. She told me I shouldn't think such horrible thoughts. When I was seven, I told my best friend, Ben, about some of the many things I dreamed up. He had told me his elaborate fantasies of being a superhero fighting alongside the ones we read about in comics. I told him stories about the macabre things people could do to each other that I came up with when I let my mind wander and other stranger things.

They sent me to a psychiatrist when Ben told our teacher. I hated that psychiatrist. I overheard him talking with my parents about sending me to a facility. They ultimately did not do that, and, for that at least, I am grateful. Instead they put me on medications. I don't remember what the medications were, but, for a time, they got me to focus. They killed my creativity and took away my ability to imagine things. I wasn't me when I was on them. So, I stopped taking them. I remember clearly when I decided I had to stop. I was only seven, and I remember that moment vividly. I couldn't live without my imagination, without that escape from the tedium of my life, from the ennui that encompassed me.

Of course, as a seven-year-old, I didn't put it in those terms. I am sure I didn't even know what ennui was then. I just felt an unrelenting boredom. I found no pleasure in the tedious cartoons and children's programming that they put on the television for me, and I had little interest in the play of other seven-year-olds. I had no friends other than those I created in my mind. So, when I was no longer able to conjure those friends in my mind, I began refusing to take the pills. The first time I tried naively telling my mother that I wouldn't take the pills, a fight started. She tried cajoling first, but when I remained obstinate, she moved on to threatening and then spanking me. It didn't take too long to get me compliant. But then I grew more sophisticated and began pretending to take them. If she wasn't watching closely, I would throw it away. When she was watching, I would make a great show of putting the pill in my mouth, but then refused to swallow the bitter thing. Once I had some liberty, I would spit it into the toilet or somewhere else it would not be found.

Once I stopped taking those accursed pills, my mind was once more my own. But I learned not to speak it. As I grew older and more sophisticated, I tried to play the part my parents so clearly wanted. I tried to wear masks to fit in with the others of my age, forced myself to play their infantile games. But I grew weary of it. By the time I was in high school, I dropped the attempt. I knew enough to tell no one of the things I imagined and the day dreams with which I filled my days. I simply withdrew into myself and read.

Mostly, I read the things my parents and teachers told me I ought to, at least when others were around. I read Shakespeare's plays and Milton's poetry. I read Dickens and learned to talk about how *A Tale of Two Cities* is filled with themes of social justice. But really,

I hated much of that. It was all far too grounded in this world of meat and dirt. I found some interest in Lewis Carroll's work. That had more imagination. The Bandersnatch intrigued me, and there were echoes of some of my own daydreams to be found through Carroll's looking glass. But it seemed still to be unreasonably bright, something written to amuse children.

When I was truly alone, I indulged in more interesting reading. I read Algernon Blackwood, Lovecraft, and William Hope Hodgson. I loved Thomas Ligotti. I also occasionally indulged in the works of Clive Barker, and my favorite was Edgar Allen Poe. When I was ready, I read philosophy as well as fiction. I would occasionally read Nietzche in front of my parents, but I did not let them know how much of his work I read. But he was not nearly nihilistic enough to conform fully to things I imagined. When I was alone, I read the philosophies of Arthur Schopenhauer. I did not agree with many of his conclusions, and his treatment of music seemed obsessive rather than reasoned, but his pessimism and his focus on suffering seemed right to me. I did not want it to be so. I would rather that the world be sunlit and beautiful, but at best that seems to be a veneer that we focus on when we are able to.

Speaking of philosophy, Nietzche famously declared that "God is dead." Was he right? When I shuffle off this mortal coil, shall I fall into the nothingness of oblivion? Can I find, if not peace, at least an end to my suffering? Or will I be cast down into a place where the fire is not quenched and the worm never dies? I know I deserve the latter, though I am hoping for the former. Oblivion is preferable to the situation I now find myself in, and even that land of fire and worms may yet be an improvement.

But I digress. I was trying to tell you what lead to this situation and why I must do this thing, even though I know it will pain you. Sacrifices must be made. When I was a teenager, I began to write down some of the fantasies that I had enjoyed internally for so long. Writing is a form of thinking, my dear, I have told you this since you were old enough to understand. The process of writing helped me to sharpen my understanding of my ideas, enhance the visions in my mind.

At first, I would often destroy my drafts. I was still afraid of what my parents would think. Those teenage texts were of a low quality anyway. But then I found the freedom of college.

That was a glorious time. I hope you are enjoying your college now. I did not precisely enjoy my time in college, but I found a new freedom. My parents no longer hovered over me, and I met many new people. I cannot say I found a kindred spirit. I never did meet another person in the flesh whom I considered a true kindred. Perhaps Poe or Lovecraft would have truly understood me. But then, perhaps, I give myself too much credit. Next to them, I am the poorest of amateurs. But I did find people that did not recoil when I mentioned my Nietzchean predilections or the appeal of certain categories of horror. Perhaps I would have been able to find such people sooner, had I not been so frightened of my parents learning and once again ensuring I took my medications. That, I could not risk.

I met your mother then. You have her raven hair and her same pale blue eyes. She had pale skin and often wore a lipstick as red as blood. Perhaps it is merely the filter of my overactive imagination, but in my memories, she invoked the image of the Grimms' Snow White. To me, though, she was no envied stepchild or even a princess, but a dark angel bringing solace in the night and a muse bringing my best inspiration. She was stunningly beautiful, but that was not important.

What was important was that she accepted me. She was quite different then from the way you knew her. She was experimental and had an interest in the macabre. If she had an interior life like mine, filled constantly with the most unusual creatures and the virtually incomprehensible lives they led, she never shared it with me. But she would listen to my descriptions without rejecting me or growing bored. She read macabre books along with me and shared my taste in movies as well. She changed after you were born. She lost her taste for the dark subjects and preferred to think about her beloved daughter. We drifted apart and fought often. Though we still loved each other, and, if may borrow from Poe, we loved with a love that was more than love.

But all of that came later. During that time in college, she was my closest confidant and the best thing in my life. Many people say that their partner is the light of their lives. She, on the other hand, helped me to enjoy and accept the darkness in mine. I sold my first novella then. I did not get much in terms of either recognition or money from it, but it was a start. It showed me that at least in certain crowds, there was a taste for my kind of brooding works, and that was all I needed to keep working.

So, I began writing far more than I used to. And by writing, I continued to immerse myself in the fantasy worlds I created in my mind. They came increasingly into focus in my mind's eye. Some of these fantasy worlds were filled with humans; some were not. My favorite was filled with odd beings that had evolved from an octopus-like creature, which I call the Calchans. They were amphibians. They preferred the water since it helped support their bodies, which were nearly boneless. They always slept in water, whether it was a natural body of water or pools they created for that purpose. But they came often onto land where it was easier to create fire, which they used to cook some of their food and to help make their tools. They had an odd form of a hive mind. Around puberty, a dozen or so would bond together in a form of marriage, and afterward, they would make all decisions together, but virtually never speak to each other. At the time, I could not figure out if they were telepathically bonded, or if they simply grew so accustomed to each other that conventional speech was unnecessary within their pod.

Figure out, rather than decide, is the appropriate word. Many writers talk about their characters running away with stories, insisting it be one way whether the author wishes it to be or not. These fantasies I created had been my companions from childhood. I had come to know the race of the Calchans, and many others, quite well. By this point in my life, they had to be the way they were, and could be no other way. Many of their ways were repulsive to humans. They considered cannibalizing the dead within their pod to be a religious duty. As creatures that lived often in water, the idea of being burned or buried was foreign to them. If they were committed to the depths of some great body of water, the other creatures within it would devour their corpses. They saw all other creatures as beneath them, so that could not be tolerated. So, they would consume their pod-mates when they died. When the pod grew too small, the dead would be consumed by other related pods. They thought this gave them a way to continue on beyond death.

I myself, found the idea repulsive. But then I am human; they are not. Is it right to judge them by human standards? Besides, the literature I wrote describing them and some of the tales of their most interesting specimens were classified as horror. Is it not the point of horror to explore the taboo and disturbing?

During and after college, I achieved some moderate success with my novels and stories. It wasn't much. I would certainly never achieve the fame or wealth that certain authors managed. I must admit, I looked on in envy at the success and popularity that was heaped upon writers like Stephen King and George R.R. Martin. They were masters of their craft and, in my opinion, deserved what they had.

Yet, still, I was jealous. That jealousy festered in me for a while, until I wrote a story about a man whose jealousy festered until it literally consumed him from within. I saw it so clearly as I wrote. In my first draft, the author was not human, but from a race of enormous insectoid creatures. He, though he was of a worker class that never reproduced, struggled to create art in a society where art was valued. How I wish our society was more like that one in my imagination. His jealousy consumed him from within, and then burst forth like an invisible parasite, seeking other failed creators to consume. I cleaned it up somewhat in the next draft. I made it an infertile human author rather than trying to explain the alien art that came to my mind. Still, the piece received some mild praise from online reviewers for carrying an unusual and alien flavor with it.

I found the process cathartic and was generally pleased with the work. I published in a small press anthology with several other authors. Within six weeks of its publication, I had largely forgotten it. Then, I received a most disturbing letter. A woman wrote to tell me that her teenage daughter, Anna, had tried to kill herself. Anna had hung herself with a silk scarf in her closet. Her mother had found her before she had died and cut the noose. She bled profusely from the nose once the pressure was released. The mother wrote to me because I was Anna's favorite author. I was flattered, in a somewhat morbid way. My story of jealousy and failed artistry was open on her desk. Her bookshelf had all of my books and most of the anthologies in which my short stories had appeared. She asked me to write to her daughter while she was in the coma, and she would read the letters to her. She hoped it might bring her some small comfort. I complied, of course, but I am not sure I had any comfort to offer.

And then you were born. When I found out your mother was pregnant, I lay awake all night. I had done that often, of course, exploring my fantastic worlds and trying to find inspiration for new stories. But this time, I thought only of the future, of how you would change it. You gave me something to live for, and you brought a pure joy into my life that I had not known before.

But you also brought responsibility. I was never a great provider. I brought in enough to tend to the needs of your mother and I, and she had been content with a somewhat Bohemian lifestyle. We were poor in terms of money, but we had our art and our appreciation for other artistic works. Now, we had another member of the family, and your mother wanted you properly cared for.

Once you were old enough to enter daycare, she put aside her own work as a painter and instead took a more conventional job in an office as an insurance agent. She was kind enough not to make me get a conventional job, but she expressed a concern at my fairly meager earnings that hadn't been there before. Her tastes also changed. She lost her taste for anything dark or strange, especially when they dealt with children. She grew, fairly quickly, to dislike reading my work. And yet, she supported me still, and loved me still. Her love, her support, her mere presence had a palliative effect on my soul.

She encouraged me to move on from horror into fantasy or even literary writing. She said she wanted me to write something that you would be able to read without being disturbed. I tried that, but it felt so unnatural. I had some meager commercial success, but it never felt right to me. So, I swiftly returned to the strange worlds that I had visited in my mind since childhood. They were weird, and at times nightmarish, but to me they felt like home.

And then I lost her. The love of my life was wretched away from my arms by the most mundane, banal event possible. She died in a car crash. I was devastated. I cannot claim I had ever been a particularly good father, but then I became the only parent you had. I strove against the travails of raising a young daughter alone. More by fortune than skill, I seem to have succeeded. Either that, or you succeeded in raising yourself; I am not certain which. But whatever the cause, you became a most remarkable young woman. You have your mother's relentless intellect and seem not to have inherited the fancies which both enliven and torment me.

I, naturally, continued to write. If anything, without the anchor that your mother provided me, my flights of fantasy became even more intense. My characters became even more alive to me and took on greater personalities of their own. I wrote then of Fnarthix, the Calchan gladiator that became a king and then conquered other lands to become an emperor. I realized while writing his saga that they were truly telepathic, and it was through a perversion of this telepathy that Fnarthix and his pod fully enslaved members of other pods. He was a great and terrible all-conqueror whose will to power was relentless.

I also started drinking then. If it were not for you, I am certain I would have drunk myself to death, or at least into a wretched state. Perhaps that would have been better. I watched you grow, and you remained the only hint of sweetness in the bitter feast my life had become.

Writing this, I feel it is in some ways pathetic. Of course, the loss of a spouse is a terrible pain that gnaws at the soul and tears at the heart. Anyone who feels otherwise cannot be said to have loved their partner. C.S. Lewis, writing about the loss of his wife, wondered if it is ever possible to return to normalcy after losing a truly loved one. But even if normalcy is impossible, a strong man, still in the prime of his life, should be able to recover from it, should he not? I do not think I ever did or will. Rather I retreated into drink and my grotesque flights of fancy and still have not recovered. Only you gave me any reason to even try.

I wrote some of my best work during this time, at least in my own opinion. In fact, I would say I had something of a literary incontinence; I simply could not stop. The visions were insufferably vivid, and I felt compelled to write them. I still gained only an inkling of commercial success, just enough to keep us fed, but I did get some praise from critics of darker materials who claimed I was original. Some of the otherworldly architecture I described in my pieces was said to be mind-bending.

I once got an email from an artist who read some of the work I created in this time. He created illustrations inspired by my work, especially the incomprehensible architecture I described. He created some impressive pieces, but none of them capture the truly alien aspects of what I saw in my mind. I do not know if that was my failing for not describing them well enough, or his for not being able to capture them.

But then you moved out. I was quite proud of you when you went off to college. I am still very proud of you. For all that I have created, you bring me the most pride. But when you left and stopped needing me, I had little reason to care. I threw myself wholly into my work.

And that is when it really started. I had always felt like the characters in my mind were other entities, that I was watching and then describing what I saw more than creating something new and original. But that was just the way it felt to me, and many writers talked about characters taking on a life of their own. But then, one of my characters began to speak to me.

Fnarthix began editorializing for me, addressing me by name. Many authors talked about their characters speaking to them, so I didn't think too much about it. It was new for my characters to directly address me, but they had always felt like their own beings. I even had thoughts it was reaching a new stage in my growth as an author. He kept trying to persuade me to put a better spin on the things I was writing about him, and he wanted me to focus on writing about him instead of any of the other characters. I, of course, laughed it off and wrote about the things that I envisioned. No one likes a Mary Sue after all.

But then I went to edit one of my short stories and found that it was in line with what he had told me to write, instead of being what I had envisioned and what I thought I had written. This annoyed me, but I assumed I had just done some of my editing after I had been drinking too much and didn't remember it. So, I stopped drinking. That was hard, but I was willing to make far greater sacrifices than that for my art.

But it kept happening. Time and again, I would go back to continue working on a piece and find that some of what I thought I had written was far more favorable to Fnarthix. It annoyed me to the point that I decided to work on different projects for a while. But that is when it got worse. Fnarthix appeared in my dreams and when I was awake, first insisting I return to writing for him. And then he began telling me to do odd things. He still won't tell me why. Sometimes he does me the courtesy of evading the questions, sometimes he merely reiterates the commands when I refuse. I refuse them, of course, but then I often find I have done what he asked anyway.

Last week, he told me to get violet paint and thin brushes. I ignored him and went out to the movies. It's rather lonely going to the movies by yourself, even when you are surrounded by other people. But when I awoke the next day, there was violet paint and several brushes in a closet. By that point, I seriously considered seeing a psychiatrist. But what would they do to me? They would almost certainly give me pills, and I loathe the very thought. The prosaicness of life would destroy me if it did end my ability to experience these other worlds. And what would I be if I could no longer write and create?

I disposed of the paint and the brushes. He told me to get them again and then to paint the deck in the backyard with an intricate pattern I am not certain I could manage. I finally told him to leave me alone. I could write about other things, perhaps even take a short break from writing. I locked myself in the house and drank as I binge-watched some ridiculous TV. I know, I have told you many times that television is a vice that rots the mind and is best avoided, but it seemed a simply enough way to distract myself. I drank and then took a sleep aid before going to bed. When I woke up, there was paint under my fingernails. I rushed out to the back and found the symbols painted on the deck, complete with elaborate flourishes and arabesques.

In something of a fit, I grabbed a hatchet we purchased for that camping trip we never took and reduced the deck to shards. My head was pounding from a hangover, and I returned inside to slump on the couch. My fingers trembled. And then his voice came to me again. It seemed to come from everywhere, and I remember precisely what it said: "It will be better for you if you cooperate. Now, repaint my symbol. Then I will have one more task for you." I tell you he said that, but he didn't, truly. Not in words. He never speaks to me in words. They are more impressions, feelings. But those impressions are quite precise. None of his people could speak English of course, but I have always known their intentions and been able to render them clearly enough.

He still will not tell me why, but I have my suspicions. They say Alexander wept when he had no more worlds to conquer. Fnarthix dominates his world with an iron hand, but he is still young by their standards. He still hungers for more. I cannot allow him to continue, not while you live. What I will do when I send this message to you, I do for you and the world.

You might not believe me; I know this. You might think that Fnarthix is a character I created. In some ways, that would be more flattering to me. I do not think that is true, but if it is, then what of it? Even if this is a creation of my own mind, it is one I can no longer tolerate, one that will not let me find peace. Either way, this must end. I only hope it does not cause you too much pain.

Farewell, my dearest Lenore.

XOXOXOXOXOXOXOXOXOX

About the Author

Timothy A. Wiseman is an attorney in Las Vegas, focusing on business and intellectual property matters. In the scant time he isn't working, he practices Brazilian Jiu Jitsu and spends time with his wife and three children. He occasionally writes dark fiction when he should be sleeping.

THE CRIER

Jason L. Kawa

The rumble of the subway echoed up through the entrance and onto the street above. Carrie, tired and exhausted, knew she'd just missed it by the fading sound. She watched as the few straggling passengers slowly ascended the steps onto the darkened late-night street above. Although it was already 2 a.m., the street still had a few people wandering about. Some were just getting off work; others were just going to work. And still others, the ones like Carrie, were out and about on the social call.

"Shit," she said, pausing and running her hands through her long, brown hair.

Now she'd have to wait for the next train. But given the time of night, it could be a while. The New York City subway ran twenty-four hours a day, seven days a week, but the hours of midnight to five in the morning were maintenance time. Trains were often spread out, delayed, or rerouted all together, and there could be long gaps in service. Still opting not to pay for a taxi, she dutifully walked down the stairs into the underground station, holding on to the faintest hope that it wouldn't be too long.

"Fucking heels," she moaned, carefully taking each step one at a time. The scanner beeped as she swiped her metro card, indicating an improper read. She tried again, but it resulted in another failure.

"Goddammit! Why'd I drink so much again?" she muttered, trying to steady her hand and swipe slowly. It took her three more tries to get the proper read.

Clumsily pushing the waist-level bar and stepping through the turnstile, she nearly tripped over her own two feet.

"Whoa…fucking heels." She cursed her footwear choice and let out a hiccup reeking of bourbon. Peering up and down the platform, she saw there was no one else waiting. She walked over to the ancient wooden benches in the middle of the platform and sat down on the cleanest spot she could find. She let out a deep sigh followed by another gagging burp.

"Hold it in there," she said, putting her left hand up to her mouth, her right fist gently rapping on her chest. Squeezing her eyes shut and holding her breath for a few seconds, she felt her stomach settle. She leaned back, opened her brown eyes, and let out another long, sleepy sigh.

Carrie sat there for a little while, staring off into the dark vortex-like nothingness of the tunnel, a long blank expression filled her face. Thinking about her life, about the bender she had been on as of late, she wondered if she was starting to develop a serious problem. This was the seventh straight night of inebriation and staying out way too late — several of which had been good old *drinking-alone* nights. Overall, she figured she'd been sober for only four or five days in the past month, and she'd called-in sick at work so many times, she was probably on the verge of being fired. This was no way for a thirty-six-year-old to live.

But in truth, most of the places she frequented those days were the types of wild bars and clubs where the younger, college-aged crowd could be found, not the kinds of places her peers would've been found socializing. But she enjoyed the rush of letting loose and acting much younger, even if it was beginning to take a toll on her body. Her hands shook most of the time, her stomach was continually upset, and her eyes looked perpetually tired from lack of decent, sober sleep. She knew very well that this lifestyle was rapidly destroying her, but in her mind, the drinking seemed to help numb the pain locked inside. The pain of her child that never was, and the pain of her failed marriage.

Thinking for a moment of her ex-husband, about how much she still loved him, and how much she knew he still loved her, she remembered how she pushed him away after the loss of their unborn child and the messy divorce that followed. That was the beginning of the dark path in her life, and now she was unsure if she'd ever find her way out, to find the light at the end of the tunnel.

The thoughts made her head spin even worse. She leaned over and took a few deep breaths, trying to rid her mind of the images and again settle her stomach.

Sitting back straight, she scanned the platform; still not another soul to be seen. Then again, two o'clock in the morning was not the busiest time for people to be meandering about this neighborhood. With two hours left till the 4 a.m. last call, it was a bit abnormal for Carrie to be heading home at this time. But tonight, she just didn't feel up to it, even though she'd been receiving some welcomed attention from an attractive younger bar patron. Tonight, she only wanted to go home and sleep it off — maybe sleep forever.

"How long is this fucking train going to take?" she mumbled. *I'm going to need the bathroom soon.*

She got up and walked over to the edge of the platform, peering down the tracks. No sign of headlights on the way. The heat coming out of the tunnel choked her breath and made her feel dizzy. A loud automated message broke the platform silence. It was one Carrie had heard a countless number of times in the city subway stations, one with an overly enthusiastic voice warning patrons to "stand clear of the platform edge." She instinctively backed away from the yellow warning track running along the edge. She knew someone in her condition shouldn't stand so close, especially with nobody nearby to help.

Backing up until she was leaning against the platform wall, she heard another announcement over the loudspeaker. This time it was a prerecorded subway service message. A man's uninterested voice announced, "Attention passengers." Carrie listened intently as the message instructed that "due to maintenance work, the 1 and 3 trains are not running in either direction between so and so stations and so and so hours. For service..."

She stopped listening.

"Dammit," she said aloud, knowing that with the 1 and 3 trains down, it only left the 2 train, which normally passed this station on the middle express tracks. However, luckily for her it was after midnight, and the 2 would be local, stopping here to pick her up.

Letting out a deep breath in frustration, her mind wandered back to the wreck of her life. Carrie didn't want to dwell on it anymore, so she tried to think about something, anything else — good times, friends, family. However, it didn't work; the thoughts were bubbling deep beneath the surface, demanding to come above, and her mind steered back toward them like an insect attracted to a flame. Then, out of nowhere, she heard something. Something weird but yet familiar was coming from the darkness of the tunnel. It was very faint, but it almost sounded like a baby's giggle.

"What the hell was that?" she said out loud. Just as quickly as the sound appeared, it was gone. Standing motionless for a few moments, Carrie listened as best she could, but there was only silence.

Jesus Christ, I must be going crazy.

Wondering for a moment if she was, in fact, beginning to hear things that weren't there, she looked down the tunnel again, but the mysterious sound didn't resume. She started back toward her bench to wait. Then, as if on cue, the sound started up again. Now she was sure that it was, in fact, real and she wasn't imagining things. The noise became clearer, and it still sounded like a baby giggling.

That sound must be coming from the tunnel. But how could that be? She sat down, wondering. *Nobody in her right mind would take a baby into a subway tunnel.*

"Right?" she asked herself

A sickening thought ran through her. *What if someone had taken the baby down there for a reason? What if it had been kidnapped?*

She walked back over to the platform edge but couldn't see anything.

Maybe a homeless person is down there with her baby? That was a more likely scenario. *Maybe she came down here because it's much warmer than the street above. Maybe this is her home.*

The noise continued in the darkness.

"Hello? Is anybody down there?"

Immediately, she felt like an idiot. *What if it's a damn murderer? Now he knows I'm here!*

The baby's giggling stopped.

A slight breeze began to pick up, and a rumbling sound grew. A train was approaching the station but on the other side.

"Son of a bitch!" she muttered.

The subway rolled into the opposite station. Carrie thought about yelling over to the train's operator and warning him about the sound she heard in the tunnel. But before she got the chance, the doors closed, and the air-brakes released, allowing the train to creep forward. Watching the train's lights illuminate the area where she was sure the sound had been emanating from, she strained to see the source. There was nothing there to see, nothing except the massive steel columns holding up the tunnel ceiling. The train continued to move away and the rumbling faded. The passengers who had just departed were already scurrying up the opposite stairwell. Carrie was alone once again. She listened a while longer, but there was only silence

I should just go get a cab and call it a night.

Just as she was about to head toward the stairs, it resumed. However, this time the sound was different. It was now a baby crying.

At first it was soft, as if the baby was making a slight fuss, but then grew louder and more enunciated. Carrie stopped and turned back. The sound was still coming from a place within the darkness of the tunnel.

"Is anybody down there?" Carrie yelled toward the crying, worried that something was, in fact, wrong. The sound of a baby crying and in potential danger would typically draw most people to help, so Carrie naturally started to walk toward the source. Passing the columns, she grabbed hold of each one for balance and reassurance. The crying continued, taking on an element of pain and urgency. She picked up her speed.

Before she knew it, she was at the end of the platform where the banged-up gate that read *Danger – Do Not Enter* and a small access ladder to the tracks were located. Looking at the warning on the gate, scared and unsure of what to do, Carrie paused. She looked back down the station platform for a security camera she could possibly wave at to summon help, but the only one she had seen was way back at the turnstile entrance. With more than 450 stations, the New York City subway was still behind in installing advanced surveillance systems in many of the smaller locations. They only seemed to care about catching those who don't pay the fare.

Shit, this station is too small and doesn't see enough tourists to be considered a terror risk.

The crying didn't stop and seemed to be coming from some ways into the tunnel.

"Hello? Are you hurt?" she called out. "Do you need help? Please answer me!"

There was no answer save for more crying.

She thought about running up out of the station and trying to find a cop to alert about the situation. But then she considered that would take a while, and in the meantime, a train could come down the tracks, putting the little thing in danger.

Pushing gently on the gate, it opened with a loud metallic creak like a rusty old sign swinging in the wind. The trespasser alarm that would've normally emitted an ear-piercing scream similar to that of a smoke alarm had evidently been disabled by subway workers and never rearmed, which didn't surprise Carrie one bit. She looked down at the ladder. It was barely wide enough for a five-year-old to descend, let alone a full-grown woman wearing high heels who has had too much to drink.

How the hell do those big track workers climb down this fucking dinky little thing?

However, after coming that far, she knew what she must do. Grabbing hold of the top handrails, she carefully and steadily placed her feet on the rungs. Taking a deep breath, she began the descent toward the tracks. The smell down there was awful. The end of the platform had always been a favorite urinating spot for vagrants, homeless, and drunks alike. Carrie even remembered a time not so long ago when she herself resorted to squatting down in the shadow of a corner not dissimilar to this one. She forced herself to hold her breath the rest of her descent.

"This is crazy; this is crazy. What am I doing?" she whispered.

Slowly and carefully, she stepped down from the ladder onto the hard ground of the tunnel floor, instantly tripping over the track rail, but she was able to right herself at the last second.

"Dammit" she said. The crying again grabbed her attention. "Hello? I'm coming to help you...Please say something so I can find you!"

No answer.

She walked along the side of the tracks but abruptly stopped.

"Where the hell is it?" she asked herself, looking around. "Fuck, what side is it on?"

She, of course, was referring to the extremely dangerous 750-volt electric *third rail*, which supplied power to the trains.

"There you are, you fucker," she said as she spied it running about a foot to the side of the right track rail.

Stepping closer to the other end of the track to avoid the danger, she continued on her way. Looking up at the surrounding tunnel walls, she saw they were covered in both old and new graffiti alike. Some of the beams and columns had illegible writing over every square inch. She wondered what the writing said.

Maybe they are people's names? Maybe they were messages to someone? Maybe they're warnings…

Carefully looking at each step, Carrie moved along slowly. The dull tunnel bulbs barely provided enough light to see the ground in front of her. Out of the darkness, a rat jumped out in front of her.

"Yuck!" She startled at the sight of it.

Carrie, having lived in the city for a good deal of her life, had lost most, if not all fear of rats and many other creepy-crawly critters. She continued moving along. The fat, gray rodent paid no attention to her and scurried back along the wall, into a crack, and then disappeared. The sight of the rat gave Carrie a weird feeling, a feeling that she was now in *their* territory; *she* was the unwelcome intruder. Shivering at the thought, she pushed it off and staggered on her way.

Hesitantly moving further down the tracks, she crossed the point where the station light cut off, and she entered into deeper darkness. With each step forward, the darkness increased, with the only source of light being the few emergency lights located at distant intervals.

She stopped and looked back toward the bright station lights behind her. They reminded her of a city far off in the distance. A feeling of loneliness passed over her. She shrugged it off and continued, the only sounds being the strange crying and the click of her own heels.

What am I doing? This is how a damn horror movie begins!

She never realized how uneven the tunnel floor and tracks were until that moment when she was trying to walk on them.

The crying was just a few yards ahead of her.

"Are you hurt? Is somebody there?" she asked in a calm voice. Perhaps some awful person had brought the little thing down there and left it to die. She'd heard stories of scared young mothers abandoning their newborns, but it was hard to fathom someone actually coming all the way down into the subway to do a thing like that. Now she was close enough to where she could zero in on the source of the crying, but she still couldn't see anyone.

"Can you hear me? I'm here to help, but I can't see you," Carrie said.

Then, in the little bit of light coming from the small tunnel bulbs, she saw it move.

The large shadow scuttled from the middle express track area where it was the darkest onto the one in front of her. It glided sleekly between the columns and then quickly darted back over to the track on the opposite side of the tunnel without making a sound. Carrie couldn't quite make out a shape; all she saw was a black mass. Whatever it was, it looked big.

Is that a person carrying the baby?

Watching it silently shoot back across the express tracks, taking notice of how smoothly it moved, a sudden chill ran down her spine and filled her body with icy dread. For the thing ahead of her moving about silently was far too massive and fast to be human. In fact, now it was beginning to take on form and appeared to be walking on all fours, like an animal. She saw what looked like four dark legs pumping up and down. The front legs were bigger and more pronounced than the back, and the dark body was large like that of a bull. Then the eyes — the bulbous eyes were red, set far to the sides of the head, which was huge and somewhat of a deformed triangular, almost crocodilian shape. At the same time, it seemed to change shape and form as the mass moved about the tunnel.

Carrie, frozen with terror, could not move or even breathe. She just stared at the shadow as it stopped directly on the track in front of her, its red glare meeting her own. The crying continued to grow louder with each passing second. The sounds were coming from the thing, the beast.

The dark mass took a few steps toward her, slowly at first, but then steadily picking up speed and confidence. Carrie started backing up but tripped and fell down. Able to quickly get back on her feet, she saw the thing still advancing.

Now knowing that this thing, this shadow, was where the crying sound was emanating from, Carrie no longer wanted to hang around to figure out why.

"Stay away!" she yelled, but the thing did not heed her command and continued its march toward her.

Turning, she ran full speed back down the way she came. The crying sound followed. Its footsteps were right behind her. She was too scared to turn back and look.

Carrie ran down the middle of tracks, away from the shadow and back toward the safety of the station platform. Not seeming to move fast enough in her heels, she tossed them off and ran barefoot, completely ignoring the sharp metal and debris that littered the tunnel floor. Seeing that she was now only a few feet from the end of the station, Carrie headed toward the ladder. The thing pursuing her was too close; it would have her before she could ascend a single rung. So, she kept on running, toward the middle of the station, in hope that someone would be there to help her.

Suddenly and unexpectedly, the dark mass stopped dead in the spot where the bright station lights flooded the tunnel entrance. It wouldn't come any further; it just stood there huffing and snorting. Whatever this thing was, it didn't want to enter into the light of the station.

Carrie, finally looking back over her shoulder took notice of this. She slowed down and stopped running.

What's it doing? She gasped for breath.

The beast's wild crying continued, but it couldn't come any closer. It was stuck there, pacing back and forth like an angry lion.

Maybe I'm safe here? Maybe it's stuck?

"Oh God, somebody help me!" she yelled out, desperately hoping for someone to be on either station platform, but there was no such luck.

What the hell is going on here? Where is everyone?

She looked around at the platform and the subway tracks trying to figure a way out. Stepping up onto the track rail and putting her arms onto the ledge, she attempted to hoist herself back onto the platform. But the base to the ground was more than five feet high, and at five-foot-four, she could barely reach over it. Still, she jumped and tried to push up with her arms, but the height was just too much. To make matters worse, the edge protruded out several feet, so she couldn't even get a grip with her toes to scramble her legs up. Hanging there in midair for a few seconds, her fingers slipped, and she fell backward down onto the tracks, the impact knocking the wind out of her.

For a few moments, Carrie contemplated just lying there, staying right in that spot until the next train pulled into the station and finished her off. The crying jolted her back to reality. She got up to her feet and dusted off her clothes. Without warning, her head started to swim from the rush of adrenaline and alcohol.

"No, not now," she said.

She tried to lean on the platform ledge, but her stomach continued to do somersaults. Buckling over, she gagged and vomited all over the tracks. On the other end of the station, the quiet crying stopped, as if the creature down there was trying to figure out what had just happened. Wiping the tears from her eyes and standing back up, she again yelled out, "Will someone please help me?"

Looking at her surroundings once more, Carrie contemplated her predicament. Then it dawned on her; she could run down to the other end of the station to reach the ladder on that side. Thinking about kicking herself for not realizing this sooner, she turned to head in that direction. However, something caught her attention. She noticed that the crying had stopped. She halted and looked back in that direction. The thing was gone.

Did it just give up and leave? Could I have imagined this?

She wondered for a moment, and then she saw it hadn't left at all, but was once again coming towards her. The large black mass was now crawling along the bottom side of the platform, using the shadow created by the overhang to shield it from the bright station light. It was headed straight for her, making an odd rattling, clicking sound.

The beast moved like a spider, with the front arms and back legs lifting high in the air before coming down over the front and torso of the body. The hands and feet on the lower side gripped the steel rail of the subway track, creating a dull clinking sound. It had elongated, claw-like fingers on the hands, each easily twelve inches long. The eyes continued to glow like embers, and they were trained straight on her. Carrie screamed and turned, trying to reach the other end of the station before it could catch up to her.

Although the distance to the other ladder was only about fifty feet, it felt like an eternity for Carrie. Finally reaching the end, she went to grab the ladder, but there wasn't one for her to grab onto; it was gone. Dumbfounded, Carrie stared at the twisted heap of metal; the ladder appeared to have been ripped right off from the platform edge, the cold steel shining where it was torn apart.

"No. No. No!" Carrie cried out, her voice trembling with fear and confusion. She looked back, and the beast was right there, almost ready to spring upon her. There was nowhere left to go, except further into the tunnel. Turning around, she fled deeper into the darkness.

Carrie ran and ran, but the crying kept getting closer and closer. There was no way to outrun the sound, no way to escape the labyrinth. Any second now, it would grab her. The terrible realization came across her mind that this was exactly what the beast wanted her to do — to travel further into the hot tunnel into its lair. She felt she couldn't go on much further. The alcohol was still streaming through her body, making her sick and dizzy. On top of it all, she was tired, tired of being alone, tired of the booze, tired of the loss. Most of all, she was tired of the regret that had become her life. She slowed down and stopped running. After pausing for a moment, she knelt down on the tracks, sobbing and out of breath. There was no hope; she could not escape it anymore. The crying was almost to her. She could hear its thudding footsteps right behind her back, and she could almost feel its hot breath.

Carrie turned on her knees to face her pursuer, to face her fate, her head swimming and her vision hazy. The thing slowly came toward her. She saw the black mass take shape, the glowing red eyes beaming at her. The creature stood straight up onto its back legs. It was several times taller than she was, but still sounded like a little baby crying for its mother. The sounds comforted her, took her to a place in the mind where she was warm and safe. She welcomed it with her arms outstretched.

"Come along now. Come to me," she said softly. Her mind had gone to a completely different world. In that world, she wasn't kneeling on the cold subway tracks. In that world, she wasn't afraid anymore.

The red eyes looked down, and the head cocked to the side; it was confused. The crying finally stopped.

Carrie heard its loud wheezing breath; she could smell the foul body odor. The creature's piercing red eyes continued to look down from the black, scaly face, burning all the way to her soul. She saw the mouth, now more reminiscent of the massive jaws of vicious dinosaurs she had once seen in movies but somehow more terrifying. The lips curled up in a grinning snarl. Saliva dripped from its lower jaw and rows of gleaming white razor sharp teeth with four big, pointed canines, the bottom set protruding further out than the top. The teeth twinkled like little stars in the weak tunnel light.

The beast paused for a moment, looking at Carrie as she looked straight back to it, her arms still outstretched. Its massive, shadowy head pulled back and pointed up into the air. Then, taking a deep breath that seemed to create a vacuum in the tight space, it let out a roar that sounded like a cross between a freight train and a hurricane. A roar so loud it deafened Carrie. The echo rumbled down the tracks like thunder. The sound was amazing considering the soft baby noises the monster had been making only moments before.

The Crier turned its head to the side, allowing one of the terrible eyes to look back down at Carrie. She hadn't moved, hadn't twitched a muscle.

In one quick motion, the head swooped down toward her with jaws open, teeth glimmering. The shadow let out another roar, this one even louder than the first. The hot blast blowing Carrie's hair backward. Throwing up an arm to shield her face from the shriek, she came back to the real world. Everything snapped back into focus. The creature's eyes became brighter and brighter, changing from red, to orange, finally to a blinding white light — the white light of high intensity headlamps. Carrie saw the sparks flying off the rails, heard the ear-piercing scream of metal on metal. A bright number 2 came into focus just before her. The jaws and teeth slammed shut and took on the form of shiny steel wheels — the wheels of a subway train. They were sliding straight toward her, sparks flying in all directions, the smell of burning brakes enveloping the air.

Carrie couldn't react even if she had wanted to.

As the jaws opened once more, Carrie had the sensation of flying, of being free and uninhibited. Before she knew it, the light at the end of the tunnel was before her and she was finally about to enter it.

There was no scream. Just the grinding of metal and the hissing of air as the train came to a jarring stop. Soon, everything was quiet again save for the yells of the train conductor and motorman and the squawking of radios. A faint sound echoed through the station, a faint crying. It crawled around the columns, floated up over the rafters, and around the beams, then swooped down through the darkness of the tunnel, and faded away. Deep down, further down in the darkness, a large black mass stealthily glided around the bend toward the next station, and disappeared into the shadowy depths below.

XOXOXOXOXOXOXOX

About the Author

Jason L. Kawa is an author from New York City, where he works in the production side of a major film and television studio. His story, "Merry-go-Round, Never Broke Down" recently appeared in the *Supernatural Horror Short Stories* anthology from Flame Tree Publishing. He also has a story that will appear in the upcoming anthology *What Dwells Below...* from Sirens Call Publications. Follow him at https://jasonlkawa.com/ or on Twitter at @JasonLeeKawa

PLEASED TO MEET ME

Peter Emmett Naughton

Gary was designated P4, which meant that he fell into the moderate-to-high risk category and, as such, only qualified for a policy with a steep monthly premium and a relatively modest payout. Part of his classification came from his pre-existing hypertension and a heart murmur he'd had since he was a kid, but mostly it was the smoking. He'd tried to quit every few months for the past six years, but he never went more than two or three weeks without relapsing.

In truth, it didn't make sense for him to have a personal insurance plan. It was like asking for a loan right after you declared bankruptcy; you might eventually be able to find yourself a lender, but the only deal they would offer is something that no one in their right mind would ever want. Even being in the business didn't help Gary's situation much, which was ironic considering that he only held onto the policy because of his job. Most folks weren't interested in buying insurance from a guy who hadn't invested in it himself. His ex-wife had told him to just lie about having a policy, but people could tell. It was like pretending to be into a band or a TV program that your friends were into just so you could join in on the conversation; you might know the lyrics to most of the songs or the names of all the characters on the show, but you always got tripped up by some little detail that exposed you as a poseur.

Gary hated that he'd been unable to give up cigarettes. He had at least gotten his habit to the point where he could make it through most client meetings without getting the shakes or having to excuse himself and pretend that he was going to the bathroom. If people didn't like the idea of buying insurance from a guy who didn't have his own policy, then they fucking hated the thought of buying it from someone who caused their premiums to go up simply by being in the same room with him.

Not that it mattered all that much these days. Ever since the economy had tanked, people were buying policies left, right, and center. Personal insurance was one of the few industries that actually thrived during a recession; the less people had, the more afraid they were of losing it. If Gary had learned one thing during his years in this business, it was that the only thing people feared more than being dead was being broke.

Some folks took this fear to unfortunate extremes, hoping to provide something for their loved ones, but the investigators always knew. Staged car crashes and faked workplace accidents always looked too meticulous and tidy. The real thing was generally a good deal messier and usually far less merciful for the ill-fated individuals whose policies actually paid out.

Gary often thought about the former group at night when he was unable to find sleep. It was the only part of the job that really got to him, imagining those poor lost souls who felt they were only worth something damaged or dead. He could handle the other unsavory details of his work, but thinking about the lives of those people always made his stomach tighten into a little ball.

When he closed his eyes, he could see their faces floating in front of him, and the expression they wore was always the same vacant, hollow gaze with no light reflected back, like looking into the black plastic eyes of a doll. On those nights, he wished he'd gone to law school like he'd planned, though he doubted that being a lawyer would've made him feel any better about the plight of the distraught, disturbed, and downtrodden that routinely plagued his dreams.

By the time Gary stopped for lunch, he had already sold five policies and only one of those had required any real effort on his part. Three were to young, stay-at-home moms, who all had the same trepidation over being left in the lurch by their husbands either from their spouse's untimely death or from some crippling disability.

None of them would come right out and say that of course, but they all used the same phrases.

Heaven forbid, perish the thought, if the worst were to happen, just for my peace of mind…

And they all wanted the same thing from Gary.

A safety net, a security blanket, a nest egg, an emergency fund, a little something set aside for a rainy day.

Those policies pretty much sold themselves, and Gary didn't feel particularly guilty about it because chances were that at least one of the three women would have her concerns validated, statistically speaking, though Gary could never predict who and was grateful for not knowing.

The fourth policy he'd sold to a man who had a genetic history of a rare but potentially serious upper-respiratory condition. Gary had recommended that the man go with a modified version of his own P4 policy after explaining that the long-term benefits would outweigh the initial investment should he find himself unable to work.

His last appointment that morning had been with a young stock trader who had tried to convince Gary that he didn't need a plan and was only there at the behest of his fiancée. It wasn't until Gary showed him the average cost of funeral services and various projections for extended hospital stays that he agreed to a basic life insurance policy. Garry actually thought the man would have been better served by a living will, but it was more expensive, and he didn't want to push his luck.

He only had one appointment scheduled after lunch, but it was all the way across town and would take him the better part of the afternoon just to get there. In some ways, it didn't seem worth it to burn the entire second half of his day on one potential client, but his newer leads weren't quite developed enough to act on, and it was better than going back to the office to start slogging through the endless pile of paperwork he'd generated from that morning's sales.

The address he had was on Layton Street in a part of town that he didn't frequent very often. It was located in an area that had mostly been farmland when he was growing up and had since been taken over by several large industrial parks. He didn't remember there being many residential buildings except for a smattering of lots with prefabricated residences, or manufactured dwellings, or whatever the hell they called trailer homes these days to try and disguise the fact that they were selling you an overpriced Winnebago without the wheels.

It turned out that Layton was less a road and more a glorified dirt rut with some loose stone scattered over the top to provide traction. Several times he felt his tires slip and thought for sure that he was going to spin out or dig himself in, but fortunately, there had been almost no snow that winter and the spring rains hadn't begun in earnest yet, so the ground was still fairly solid.

When he finally reached the address, it wasn't a trailer, though the size of the structure wasn't much larger than if it had been. Instead, what greeted him was a small ranch house with yellowing paint that was peeling off in strips and a roof that appeared to be missing a good number of its shingles.

He double-checked his paperwork and then stepped out of the car to verify the address on the front of the house. The screen door was ajar, hanging by only the top hinge, and the wooden door beyond it was badly battered on the bottom.

This has to be a joke, Gary thought. Someone at the office was playing a prank on him. They'd changed the address in the system and sent him to a condemned property.

He was about to get back in the car when a man opened the wooden door and poked his head out.

"Can I help you with something?" the man said.

"I'm sorry, I think I have the wrong address," Gary said.

"Who were you looking for?"

Gary had been so distracted by the house that he'd completely forgotten the name and quickly riffled through the pages in his binder.

"Sorry, I was trying to reach uh...Mr. Blakely?"

"Oh yeah, The Blakelys, real nice folks, reminded me of my parents. I bought this place from them a couple months back. I think they moved to Florida or someplace warm like that. My name's Vincent, by the way, Vincent Fodor, but everybody just calls me Vic. Is there something *I* can do for you?"

"Well Mr. Fodor..."

"Really, Vic is just fine."

"Yes, of course. Can I ask you something, Vic?"

"Sure."

"Have you ever thought much about your future?"

"Which part in particular?"

"Having stability and security as you go about planning a life for yourself. For instance, what do you do for a living?"

"I work mostly as a general contractor and carpenter, though I've been known to do some electrical and masonry from time to time."

"Let's just say something were to happen to you, and you were unable to work."

"That's not likely. I love what I do, and there ain't a thing on earth that'd keep me from it short of being dead."

"And what if that were to happen?"

"Being dead?"

"Hypothetically speaking."

"Well then, I guess I wouldn't have to worry about work any more."

"What I mean Mr. Fodor…"

"Vic."

"Right, sorry, Vic. What I was saying is that should a tragic and unexpected event occur, you'd want your loved ones to be protected."

"Protected from what?"

"Bills, bankruptcy, foreclosure, and any other financial hardships your family might suffer from your loss. Heaven knows that at such a difficult time, the last thing they should be worrying about are money troubles."

"Listen, Mister?"

"Bennett, Gary Bennett."

"Gary all right with you?"

"Please."

"Listen, Gary, you seem like a nice enough fella, but I ain't got any kids or even a wife, and my folks passed away a few years ago."

"I'm sorry to hear about your parents."

"Thanks, I appreciate that. You can see, though, that there isn't really anyone to look after."

"Even still, there's always the possibility that you could need money for yourself should you become sick or injured."

"If I'm ever that bad off, I hope someone does me the kindly gesture of puttin' a bullet between my eyes."

Gary's face turned downward in a grimace before he could stop himself.

"Sorry, that was probably a bit melodramatic." Vic chuckled softly. "All I meant is that I wouldn't want to be laid up in some hospital bed or stuck around the house doing nothing but watching TV and collecting a check. I know some folks do that, and I don't have anything against them, but I don't think I could live that way myself."

"Don't think of it as a hand out. This would be a policy that you paid for to get you back on your feet. It's just insurance like you have on your home or your vehicle."

"I get having insurance on something like a house or a truck, but having it on a person just strikes me as kinda strange. It's like placing a bet on yourself that something bad is gonna happen."

"I know how you feel Vic. Personal insurance can seem like a damned if you do, damned if you don't sort of deal. If you keep paying your premium each month and nothing happens, then you feel like you're throwing money away. But then if something does happen and you need your insurance, it can feel like you jinxed yourself."

"Does seem a bit like tempting fate."

"But if that were really true, then no one would have medical insurance or even bother going to the doctor for that matter."

"Truth be told, I'm not the biggest fan of hospitals."

"No one is, Vic, but we go because in the end, we know it's the sensible thing to do," Gary said, and suppressed the urge to scratch the back of his neck, which had begun to tingle nearly fifteen minutes ago. The throbbing at the base of his head had started five minutes ago, and he knew soon his temples would begin to pound and ache.

"Are you okay? You look a little pale."

"I'm fine; I recently quit smoking, and it's been a little rough."

"I feel you there, brother."

"How long has it been for you?"

"Just over two years, and let me tell you, it was a bitch and a half to quit."

"God, I've been trying for I don't know how long. No matter what I do, I just can't seem to shake the damn things. Every other person I know managed to give them up years ago, but I keep coming back like some damn junkie."

"Yeah, I tried a million different things until I finally found something that stuck."

"Mind if I ask what?"

"Not at all, but it might be easier if I showed you? Why don't you come on inside?"

Gary glanced at his watch. "I really should be getting back."

"Giving up so soon? You don't strike me as the type."

Gary laughed. "No, I suppose I'm not," he said and followed Vic through the askew screen door.

The inside of the house was surprisingly neat and tidy, though still worn and faded the way the outside had been. There was a long row of wooden shelves running along the top of the wall in the living room that held dozens of books; Gary scanned the spines and immediately spied several he had in his own bookcase back home.

"Expecting more of a trailer trash chateau?" Vic said seeing the surprise on Gary's face.

"Oh, uh no, I..."

"I know the place still needs a lot of work. The down payment left me pretty tapped out, and it'll be a while before I can fix it up proper, but it's coming along."

"Looks like it has a lot of potential," Gary said, instantly regretting his choice of words.

Vic took a seat at a small wooden table set into a nook at the end of the living room and motioned for Gary to do the same.

"I don't figure I'll be getting many calls from *Better Homes & Gardens* or *Good Housekeeping,* even after I spruce it up," Vic said.

"But it has good bones and a solid foundation, and, honestly, it's all the space a guy like me really needs."

"I'd probably be able to say the same about my place if it wasn't such a mess all the time."

"Now that's no way to talk."

"What, admitting that I'm a slob?"

"No, I mean the whole negative attitude. When you were selling me a minute ago you were all confidence, but the moment you started talking about yourself, it completely vanished."

"Sorry, it's a congenital condition caused from growing up in Brooklyn. Instead of putting fluoride in the water, they pumped it full of cynicism."

"I'm telling ya, thinking like that all the time will eat you up inside. Trust me on this one. I was the exact same way; always down on myself and thinking I couldn't be successful and do the things I wanted to do, but I found a way to turn that all around."

"You're not about to pull a Tony Robbins on me, are you?"

"I don't much go in for that new-age, self-help stuff, but I did find something that pointed my life in the right direction. Got me off the coffin nails and out from pumping gas."

"All right, so what's the big secret?"

"What you need to do is completely reset your system. Start over from square one."

"And how exactly do I do that?"

"I'll show you. Just let me grab something from the back. Can I get you a beer or something?"

"Normally I wouldn't during business hours, but seeing as you're my last appointment, I guess it won't hurt anything."

"That's what I like to hear," Vic said and disappeared into the kitchen.

A few moments later, he emerged with two bottles of Miller and a big bowl of pretzels. He handed one of the bottles to Gary and placed the bowl in front of him.

"Thanks."

"My pleasure. You'll have to excuse my manners for not asking sooner."

"Are you kidding? Most houses don't even offer me a glass of water."

"I'll be back in just a sec."

Gary watched Vic head down a short hallway and go through a door that he assumed led to the bedroom. He took a long pull on the bottle of Miller and let out a small sigh of satisfaction. It didn't scratch the itch the way a Marlboro would have, but it definitely helped take some of the edge off. The pretzels were the square kind that Gary had always thought resembled little pieces of woven fabric. He hadn't had them in years, but when he put one in his mouth, he instinctively probed his tongue into the tiny holes the same way he had when he was a kid.

"Pretzels and beer, the ambrosia of the gods," Vic said, walking back in from the hall.

Gary chuckled. "There *is* something about them."

Vic sat back down and placed a photo in front of Gary. The picture showed a lithe man in his late teens or early twenties with dark, close-cropped hair and sharp cut facial features wearing a pair of faded blue jeans and a white undershirt.

"That you?"

"In my younger days. Notice anything about it?" Vic said.

Gary studied the photo for a moment. "Well, you kinda look like De Niro in *Taxi Driver*, ya know, minus the mohawk."

"Don't I wish," Vic said. "Take a closer look at the left arm."

Gary inspected the photo again and saw that the left shirtsleeve was rolled up and there was a bulge protruding from it.

"Looks like you've got some smokes tucked into your shirt."

"They were much more than that. That pack of cigarettes was my constant companion, my talisman. Even when I was out of cigs, I'd keep the empty box in my sleeve until I got a new one."

"Why?"

"Because it was part of my identity. Understand that I'm not just talking about style or image here. I wasn't laboring under the delusion that I was James Dean or Jim Morrison, though I certainly admired guys like them. The cigarettes were part of my understanding of who I was and how I wanted to be perceived. When I first tried to quit smoking, it felt like there was this mental block inside my head that refused to budge, even after the nicotine had left my system. I think most people are so averse to change that they become allergic to the very idea of it."

"So then, what did you do?"

"I became someone else."

"I'm not sure I follow you."

"I invented a whole new persona for myself. Not just a version of me that didn't smoke, but a completely different guy."

"You mean like acting?"

"It goes deeper than that. You have to create someone that embodies the things you want, everything from major life goals to specific qualities and habits. Then you have to come up with a new name and a new personal history with opinions, interests, hobbies, favorite foods, everything you need to make the new you real. After you have this person set in your mind, you take their traits and make them into a mantra that you say to yourself a hundred times before you go to bed. Repeat it to yourself a hundred more times as you get ready in the morning. Say it in your car on the way to work, in the elevator, on your lunch break, at dinner, when you're watching television, say it until this new person *is* you."

"Are you *sure* you're not into that self-help stuff?"

"I know it sounds kinda strange, but trust me; it works. Just think of it like playing pretend when you were a kid. Make your list and then make believe."

"I don't know if I can."

"You're a salesman; all you have to do is sell the idea to yourself."

"Well clearly I'm not that great a salesman. I mean I didn't even manage to sell you a policy."

"Very smooth."

"I try."

"I'll tell you what. You come back here after you've stopped smoking for three weeks, and we'll work something out. Hell, maybe I can leave my meager worldly possessions to some charity."

Gary considered the proposal for several moments and then extended his hand to Vic. "All right, you've got yourself a deal," Gary said, shaking Vic's hand and assuming that he would probably never see him again.

The first list Gary came up with for his new persona read like something out of a romance novel. Charming, resourceful, clever, responsible, athletic, courteous, well groomed, and at the end of the list, he had even scribbled in handsome, as if he had some say over that. He might as well have written down super strength, x-ray vision, and the ability to fly while he was at it.

It took almost two hours and several revisions, but he finally managed to pare down the list to a set of reasonable and realistic qualities. Essentially, he just wanted to create a healthier, more personable, and overall more content version of himself, which sounded simple, but then he'd been trying to do that for years.

After leafing through the phone book for ideas and mulling it over for a while, he came up with a name for his new persona and spent the quiet moments as he was drifting off to sleep envisioning himself as his alter ego, Richard, and whispering his new litany of attributes over and over. The broad strokes were that he was a non-smoker with an active lifestyle and a positive mental outlook on life. He'd begun a modest exercise routine that consisted of jogging in the morning before work and lifting weights at a nearby gym three nights a week. He went to the library looking for anything that might aid him in his conversion. He was still leery of self-help books; perusing a few of the titles on the shelves only served to reinforce this bias, but he did find some useful tips in a couple of books aimed at business executives that were basically just updated versions of *How to Win Friends and Influence People*.

Gary integrated some of the slogans from the books into his daily mantra and began trying as Richard to apply these ideas during his client meetings. At first, he had a hard time altering his sales pitch, which had always been serious and sober, but after a few weeks, he began to get the hang of it. Soon, it became natural for him to talk about things like accident coverage and death benefits in between gabbing about his golf game or some new sitcom on TV, and people smiled right along with him as they signed up for term-life and catastrophic-injury policies.

The shift over to his new identity was simultaneously exhilarating and exhausting. Gary had always been very low-key and reserved, but Richard was Mister Positivity, all sunshine and rainbows, highlighting the silver lining on every potential dark cloud. He had become so good as Richard that if a client still wasn't biting after his initial pitch, then he could just change tact and turn into Captain Charm, making the client see how smart and wonderful they were and how important it was to protect someone as special as them.

Now that the main pillars of his new persona had been put into place, Gary started in on the finer details. He had always been a coffee addict so he decided that Richard preferred tea; he adjusted his heavily meat-centered diet over to something with more vegetables and whole grains, which he'd been meaning to do anyway. He switched the part in his hair from the left side to the right and traded in his old tan suit for a new charcoal gray one, picking out an assortment of ties to go with it in vibrant, solid colors that were worlds away from the pastel and patterned ones he'd previously worn.

And he slowly began to cut back on his smoking.

Quitting smoking made the other aspects of his transformation seem simple by comparison. Sure, he sometimes missed the cheeseburgers and the espressos, but the more he went without them, the less he noticed their absence. The exact opposite was true of cigarettes. Every time he went to reach for a smoke and found nothing there, his whole body twitched like an electric current had been run through it. He was down to a half-pack a day, which was a lot better than his former two-and-a-half pack habit, but he still felt ill whenever he thought of stopping completely.

After the first few months, he hadn't needed to repeat the other parts of his mantra to keep himself on track, but he kept saying his new name and the fact that he was a non-smoker to himself again and again like a guilty man reciting an Act of Contrition.

My name is Richard Dunmore, and I do not smoke; my name is Richard Dunmore, and I do not smoke; my name is Richard Dunmore, and I do not smoke; my name is Richard Dunmore, and I do not smoke; my name is Richard Dunmore, and I do not smoke; my name is Richard Dunmore, and I do not smoke; my name is Richard Dunmore, and I do not smoke; my name is Richard Dunmore, and I do not smoke; my name is Richard Dunmore and I do not smoke; my name is Richard Dunmore and I do not smoke; my name is Richard Dunmore, and I do not smoke; my name is Richard Dunmore, and I do not smoke...

Gary punched ten digits into his cell phone and hovered with his thumb perched above the call button. It was late, probably far too late for a phone call, and he put the cell down on the table. He shut his eyes in an exhausted wince and slowly rubbed at them with his thumb and forefinger while he drained the last dregs of coffee from the mug in his other hand and signaled the waitress for more.

It had been a long time since he'd had coffee, had been a long time since he'd felt anything like himself. The only regular reminder he had of his old self was his name stenciled on his office door, but the man who'd gotten him that new office had an entirely different name. Richard had also been the one to get him in shape to the point that the new charcoal suit he'd bought had needed to be taken in, and he'd since replaced most of his old wardrobe. As Richard, he had successfully climbed the corporate ladder at work and received two promotions over the past seven months. He'd even seemed happier as Richard, at least from outward appearances, but the cheery personality was like everything else about Richard, a high-gloss veneer that had to be continuously buffed and polished to keep its shine reflected to those around him.

Gary glanced down at his phone, the ten digits staring back at him, and let out a long, measured exhale as he pressed the call button.

It took Vic several moments to realize his phone was ringing. He didn't receive much in the way of phone calls, especially not at 3:34 in the morning on a Tuesday.

"Hello?" Vic said, his voice still groggy with sleep.

"Vic?"

"Yeah, who is this?"

"It's Gary Bennett, I don't know if you remember me?"

"Gary the insurance guy."

"Right. Look I'm really sorry to be calling you so late."

"Is this about the policy? Cause I gotta say, ignoring me for months and then phoning me in the middle of the night is a pretty odd sales strategy."

"It's not about that."

"So, what's on your mind then?"

"It's Richard."

"Who?"

"My alternate persona, the one you told me to create to help me stop smoking."

"Oh yeah, I forgot to ask how that went. Have you managed to quit yet?"

"Yes, but…"

"That's great! Seriously, congratulations, Gary."

"Listen, Vic, you have to help me. Richard's totally taken over my life."

"What do you mean?"

"Whenever I try to do anything, I can feel him watching me, and more and more often, he seems to take over completely. I have spans of hours and sometimes even whole days where it feels like I'm just a passenger in my own body, and I'm afraid that sooner or later, he's gonna give me the boot for good."

"Wow…that sounds pretty intense."

"That's putting it mildly; I'm at my wits end. How did you handle it?"

"I didn't have to."

"I don't understand? Wasn't it the same for you?"

"Not really. Honestly, when I gave you that advice, I was just trying to motivate you."

"But you said you'd followed the same kind of thing, right?"

"Well yeah, but I never had any out-of-body experiences."

"So you're basically saying that I'm some kind of freak."

"Sounds to me like you just went a bit overboard."

"It's more than that. He's so damn charismatic, and everybody loves him; he's a killer salesman, the life of the party around the office, and even management adores him. Hell, they gave me the employee-of-the-year award, and I couldn't even tell you the name of any of my recent clients, because Richard's the one who snagged them all."

"And you're afraid to give that up?"

"Hell no, I just don't know how to get rid of him."

"Where are you right now?"

"In some all-night diner at the edge of Bumsville, Idaho."

"They sell cigarettes there?"

"I dunno, maybe. Why?"

"I think you need to buy yourself a pack and light up immediately."

"How is that gonna help?"

"It's the exact opposite of what Richard would do. If you can get that wedge in, it might be enough to start edging him out."

"Maybe, but do you really think I should start smoking again?"

"I know it's not an ideal solution."

"Honestly, at this point, I am willing to try just about anything."

"Why don't you stop by my place tomorrow, and we'll see if we can figure a way to exorcise old Richard."

"What time should I come around?"

"Anytime after ten will be just fine."

"Thanks Vic, I really appreciate this."

"Sleep tight Gary. I'll see ya tomorrow.

The knock on Vic's door came at exactly 10:01.

"Good morning to you, sir. My name is Richard Dunmore, and I represent the Premium Mutual Insurance Company out of Saint Claire."

"Well hello, Richard. I've heard a lot about you," Vic said as he opened the front door. He almost didn't recognize Gary, who looked to him to have dropped at least twenty-five pounds and was now sporting a tan, despite it being the middle of winter.

"Ah yes, from my associate Mr. Bennett. It's a pleasure to meet you Mr. Fodor. My colleague indicated that you might be interested in one of our personal policies. If you wouldn't mind sparing just a few minutes of your time, I'd love to tell you about the many benefits provided by our comprehensive and affordable coverage plans."

"You can call me Vic. Please, come in."

Richard took a seat at the small wooden table, and Vic started to sit down but then stopped.

"Can I get you something to drink Richard, a nice cold beer perhaps?"

"As tempting as that sounds, I'm afraid I don't indulge during business hours."

"I see," Vic said, barely managing to repress a grin. "How about some water then?"

"That would be wonderful."

Vic turned and headed into the kitchen returning a moment later with a tall glass of ice water that he set down in front of Gary.

"Thank you," Richard said, taking a long swallow from the glass.

"To be perfectly honest, Mr. Dunmore, I'm not sure I have much use for insurance. I'm not married, and I don't really have any family around. What I'd really like to discuss with you is your business partner, Gary."

"I wouldn't call us 'partners' per say. Don't get me wrong, Mr. Bennett is a great guy, salt of the earth, really, but he does lack a bit in the motivation department. But back to what I was saying, there are many other good reasons to have a policy in place, Mr. Fodor."

"You can just call me Vic."

"Let me tell you about our three most popular packages for singles," Richard said and pulled three packets of paper from a leather portfolio and placed them in front of Vic. "There's our bronze personal plan, which provides basic limited-injury coverage; our silver personal plan, which provides additional support for living expenses and extended work absences; and our gold personal plan, which provides full catastrophic accident and injury coverage with…"

"Pardon me, Mr. Dunmore, I don't mean to interrupt, but would you happen to have a cigarette on you?"

"Oh, I don't smoke; hard to have a habit like that in my business. My only real vices are hitting the links whenever I can, a nice corned beef sandwich with spicy mustard, only on special occasions, of course, and my nighttime TV addiction," Richard said, chuckling to himself. "Say, did you see that show last night, the one with the talking dog detective? I don't know where they come up with this stuff."

"No, I missed that one," Vic said, wondering whether Gary had managed to implement his plan since the last time they'd spoken.

"Richard, can I call you Richard?" Vic said.

"By all means."

"Richard, you've done a very thorough job of laying out all the options, and I think I'm leaning towards the bronze plan, but before we get too far into that, I really need to talk to you about Gary."

"Can I be honest, Mr. Fodor?"

"Vic, please."

"Yes, of course. Vic, I think that you would really benefit from our silver or even our gold plan. Both of these plans have much more comprehensive coverage when it comes to unemployment protection, and with you being the only source of income in your household..."

"It's like I told you before. I love my job, and, short of being six feet under, I can't think of much that would keep me from working."

"I'm sorry, I don't think you mentioned your profession. What is it you do?"

"I guess Gary didn't fill you in. I'm a general contractor and carpenter."

"For someone in your line of work, I really feel that having a policy that covers on-site injury is imperative. The fact of the matter is that without some form of disability protection, you run the risk of bankruptcy should something serious happen to you while on the job."

"Really, I'm very careful."

"That's why they call them accidents, Mr. Fodor."

"Look, I can appreciate what you're saying, but for my needs I really think the bronze plan is the way to go."

"I don't mean to overstep my bounds, Mr. Fodor..."

"Vic."

"My apologies, I have an ingrained tendency toward formality in business matters."

"That's all right."

"I understand your hesitance, Mr. Fodor, but if something were to happen to you, not having the proper coverage could leave you exposed to massive debt. I'd hate to see you put in a position that could ruin you financially."

"You are persistent; I'll give you that. If you'll excuse me for a moment, I think I'm going to grab myself a beer. Can I get you some more water?"

"I'm fine, thank you."

"All right then, be back in a jiff."

Vic stood up and ambled across the floor to the kitchen, hoping that Gary or Richard or whoever the hell was in his living room didn't notice how eager he was to leave. He still thought it possible that Gary might simply be pulling his leg, but if he was, then he was doing a hell of a convincing job.

Vic grabbed a Miller from the fridge and held it against his forehead, letting the cold sheen of perspiration penetrate his skin for several moments before finally cracking it open and heading back to face his creation.

"Listen, I've been mulling it over and I really think..."

"This, Mr. Fodor, is exactly the type of situation I'm talking about."

"Gary, what the hell are you doing?"

"The fact of the matter, Mr. Fodor, is that you never know what life is going to throw your way. Having the comprehensive coverage our gold plan provides guards you against these kinds of scenarios."

"Okay, just take it easy and put the gun down."

"I'm afraid I can't do that, Mr. Fodor."

"I'll buy any plan you want, gold, platinum, whatever; just calm down, and we can start on the paperwork."

"I fear that you still don't believe me, Mr. Fodor. That you think I'm simply feeding you some hackneyed sales pitch."

"Gary, this has gone far enough. I need you to snap out of it and put the pistol on the ground right now."

"It's important to me that you understand why proper coverage is so vital..."

"C'mon Gary, you're not his puppet. You created him, not the other way around. Don't let this asshole control you."

"I'm sorry to inform you that Mr. Bennett is no longer employed with the company. I made sure of that last night after your little conversation."

"Gary, please..."

There was a deafening crack that echoed off the walls, and Vic fell backward through the kitchen archway, clutching at his chest as his legs buckled, and he crumpled onto the checkered linoleum floor.

"I told you before, Mr. Fodor, my name is Richard."

〉〈〉〈〉〈〉〈〉〈〉〈〉〈〉〈〉〈〉〈

About the Author

Peter first fell into fiction, penning stories to amuse his grammar-school classmates, which helped him overcome his shyness, but resulted in very few completed homework assignments. He was raised and currently resides in the Chicagoland suburbs with his wife and cats. His writing has appeared in *The Delinquent, Candlelight, Black Words on White Paper, Spook City, Apiary, Crack the Spine, Chicago Literati, Cemetery Moon, Pavor Nocturnus, Sanitarium, 1000words, 1:1000, Cacti Fur, The Literary Hatchet, Graze*, and the *Dark Lane Anthology*. You can visit him online and learn more about his writing at: http://ravenpen.wixsite.com/authorsite

FOOTPRINTS IN THE SNOW

Andrew Benn

In the north of Finland, where I lived for some years what seems a long time ago, there are places dark and cold that have scarcely felt the touch of humanity. Infrequently one can find a road or village amid the endless miles of forested tundra that rises slowly out of the lakes in the south toward the *Skandit*, the mighty mountains that form the spine of Norway and that adorns the reaches of Lapland like a frozen crown. Perhaps once in a generation, events of the wider world penetrate to those roads and villages, and for a while, they remain, but always they fade away into the snow, leaving nothing but footprints, all too soon covered over by fresh drifts, born aloft by the eternal, biting arctic wind.

I loved, for a while, those places of snowy isolation, where only the trees stand vigil over empty vistas of polar beauty. I moved there — as one might expect of a Briton emigrating to what is, to many, the very ends of the earth — for work. I was employed by one of the larger of Finland's many lumber companies. My duties were entirely clerical and so soul-grindingly dull I should have gone mad were it not for the walks. The town where I lived was called Salla; it sits not far from the Russian border and about three-fifths of the distance between Helsinki and the windblown peaks of the *Skandit* on Finland's northern reaches. The forests there are very old and the people very quiet. Kind, but quiet and reserved in a way striking even compared to their compatriots, deeply proud as they all are of their legendarily stolid dourness.

The walks I mentioned were first necessitated by the short distance from my home, a plain, warm building of one story in the traditional Nordic style, and my office. Most of my colleagues drove the few kilometers to the regional headquarters of our company, but I always walked. At first, it was out of a simple desire to see more of my new home, but subsequently, they, and the many longer rambles I took on my days off, became nothing less than my lifeline in a sea of mediocrity and drudgery.

Those walks were enchanting. In summer, they were warm and pleasant, in spite of the perennial scourge of the mosquitoes that rose from the marshy ground in voracious swarms. In the end, I took to driving during the worst of such confluences, but for the rest of the year, I always refused any other mode of transport than my own booted feet, no matter the weather. Not for nothing does all the best winter clothing come from Scandinavia, and suitably attired, one can walk for hours through that land of icy silence, safe within a bubble of warmth, insulated from the chilling emptiness that is all around you. But at that time, I thought differently. Those dark mornings and freezing blasts of arctic rain held for me nothing but beauty. I found tranquillity in every falling drop, in every glistening pine tree, a permanence that spoke to me of something larger, older, and more real than any of the fleeting tracks left my humanity upon this world we call our own.

In winter though, the road took on a new and wholly different character. The snow that covered everything with a softening, soothing blanket glowed in the moonlight and was more hauntingly beautiful than anything I can describe or even understand. There is a permanence to that place, even when snow does not lie heavily on everything, but when it is draped in that shroud, it gleams silver in the short boreal days and glows softly blue when the polar stars shine down on it. That land is nothing less than the frozen kingdom of Narnia that flowed from the pen of the gifted C.S. Lewis, though back then, it held none of the fear or dread of that bewitched realm. In the preternatural cold, ice crystals sprout from every surface and trees become glass statues — half groaning, half grinding in the cold breezes. Drifts of snow as high as my waist pile up in wind-blown banks like embankments, and moving through them is hauntingly like wading through deep water, pushing forward with each step and sending up sprays of sparkling white. I think we forget — we who do not live in places such as this — the kinship that is shared between water and snow. There is a permanence to the sea, and the same is true, I think, of the endless snowbound places in this world.

Those walks are what first made me think about footprints. I was not the only pedestrian on that road or on the many tracks and pathways that cross the voids between the arterial roads and railways. There were dog-walkers, hunters, hikers, tourists, and those who engage in the peculiar pastime of Nordic walking. That, added to the mess of tire tracks and treads carved into the compacted snow of the road by the continuous procession of industrial logging vehicles, turned the snowy ground before my feet into a long, confused record of a time now passed. As I took those tracks more and more frequently, I started to recognize the footsteps as I passed them. Though I had no names to attach, at length, it felt like seeing old friends each day: who had been there, when, where, had they met anyone, had the dog behaved? All these mundane yet delightfully real events, lifetimes, were recorded for a few months a year, for a while, on the surface of that frozen ocean that is the perma-frosted arctic.

I had already lived in Salla for nearly four years when I noticed that strange thing, which I now must relate. It was, as these things often are, so small at first but grew like a monster from childhood, quietly but menacingly until there was nothing else, and I had, I now realize, no choice in what I did. It has taken all the beauty from this place; it has taken the wonder and replaced it with fear, and in the dark, the wind howls like laughter and the stars seem distant and indifferent to the plight of humanity. What I noticed was only this: that every day, every morning, at the same place, a single set of solitary footprints left the road and struck out determinedly into the dark depths of the snow-bound forest. For the first week, or two perhaps, it was of only passing interest; there were any number of reasons for what was, after all, only a slight anomaly. There are hunters, bird-watchers, even dog-walkers who for one reason or another kept very methodical schedules and follow a single routine day in and day out. Though I could not know if they had been there over the summer, nor could I recall if they had been there the previous winter, there was still little grounds for unease. Yet unease I certainly began to feel as each day I drew close to that place where that single set of prints left its fellows to venture into an area I knew well enough was uninhabited and for the most part untraversed.

As the days passed and the winter grasped more tightly the around the land, the usual wonder and excitement I had felt seemed to be rapidly evaporating; my recreational walks became more infrequent, and when I did venture out, even during the brief hours of daylight, I found myself constantly walking with hunched back. As if studying the ground before my feet, as if searching for some sign or mark in the snow which felt again like it was stretching out before me in an endless white blanket of which time and human existence could only disturb but the uppermost layer. I don't know where these feelings came from, or why they attached themselves so firmly to those footprints that departed the crowd with such maddening regularity. Perhaps it was their abrupt departure; perhaps it was that I could not identify them, that disturbed thoughts already lurking behind my childish wonder at the new and fantastical.

I did, more than once, stop to bend down and scrutinize those tracks as they mounted the gradual bank on the northward side of the road before disappearing between the heavy-laden boughs and beyond my sight. They were stubbornly unrevealing, being always too distorted by the blowing dust of the fresh falling snow, and I found myself longing for a break in the crisp, cold weather so that a partial thaw would preserve them better through the long windy nights. Such a morning never came, however, and I was always confronted by the same nondescript boot-prints already partially erased by the march of polar time.

I do not know, either, what prompted that final pause at that hateful place, that last lingering that lead me down a path I now see has, and never has had, an end. Not that can be reached by the living at least. It is true the prints had been growing on my mind; the few people that I had come to know even slightly had marked the uncharacteristic change in me, for I had been remarkable, even among the locals, for my love of the Siberian winters of their homeland, and the haggard, even haunted expression they said I sometimes wore unnerved them greatly. My walks to and from work had ceased to be a pleasant respite from reality and now were, from their commencement, entirely focussed on that distant point, about halfway along the road, where I knew the prints would be waiting. The anxiety intensified as they drew nearer, but would not recede once I had managed to force myself, eyes fixed on my own booted feet, to pass them by. Instead, my neck would prickle under the thick scarf in a way that sent shivers of fear and danger through by my whole body so that it was not until I turned the corner into town or off the road toward the office that I could feel anything approaching calm.

My work suffered, noticeably, and it was while walking back from being sent home early that I made my final stop before that trail that struck out so accusingly into the unknown. It was already late afternoon, and the sun was setting low behind the horizon of treetops at my back when my determined stride faltered. My eyes, which I so religiously kept away from the sight that so consumed me, had strayed, and I glanced down to see what I knew awaited me, and without thinking, I stopped walking. I have said I do not know now why I did, though I am dogged by the feeling that I did know, in that moment of indecision, why I stopped, and why I turned, and why I struck out with those accursed tracks and abandoned the living world forever.

What I felt when I finally left the road behind and started to follow these prints was complex: the crossing of a previously insurmountable mental barrier blending elation and trepidation, even though I knew the area well. I had sketched in my mind the environs likely to be traversed by those tracks, the paths they might connect with, the thickets and patches of frozen water they would have to avoid, and I was, for a while, encouraged that my assumptions seemed to be borne out as the prints before me wove between the several dense, ancient clumps of silver elms and evergreen firs that formed reassuring landmarks in the middle of the breathless excitement. I noticed, however, that though the tracks seemed to be shadowing the courses of the familiar paths, their route was such that neither they nor I were visible from those paths. Being always at least partially concealed by a drift of snow or a fortuitous convocation of leaning trunks, I was forced to conclude that whoever it was that made the trail that I now followed had wanted to avoid being seen, despite the stark emptiness of the whole frozen world around me, so that the feeling of dread never wholly left me.

It did not take long for that dread to overtake any other sensation as I continued to stumble and push through deeper drifts of snow and the light faded. I had expected, or perhaps hoped, that the trail would be short and that it would end with some house or at least rejoin a more frequented thoroughfare and dispel a little the mystery that had grown so large in my imagination. But it did not. As the polar night drew in around me, the tracks saw no sign of slowing but pushed determinately onward, leaving a deep carven trench in snowbanks that skirted around arboreal landmarks, which, it slowly dawned on me, I no longer recognized. I had, without realizing it, passed beyond the limit of my lengthy expeditions and was now blazing a trail through entirely new and unknown regions of wintery night. Regions that held no pleasant memories or connotations for me, and trees loomed out of the gloom like jeering skeletons.

The cold, too, became intense. It leaked through my trousers and boots, robbing me of feeling in my feet. My breath froze in the weave of my scarf, and I could feel the snow collecting on my eyelashes. Usually, thanks to the aforementioned quality of Scandinavian winter clothing, one sweats despite the sub-zero temperature, but then, with the wind howling all around me, and the trailing twigs seeming to quiver in anticipation as I passed, even those specialized garments were no proof, and no part of me remained warm. All sense of self-preservation evaporated as I continued to follow those tracks, which plunged ever onward into unknown and unimagined regions of cold and forgotten earth. I think my body would have given up long before this without the resolute will which drove me to continue. My legs ached and my ears screamed as the wind whipped through my thick woolen hat and licked them with tongues of ice. My fingers I would rather not think about. It all seemed so meaningless compared to the sight before me. The footprints in the snow that never faltered, striding on and on with unwearied feet toward some destination beyond anything humanity has dreamed of.

I confess I did not think much of that destination, that goal toward which these prints seemed now to be hurrying. For me, there was only the trail. I squinted through the ethereal gloom of an aurora, making the snow appear like deep blue velvet, but I had eyes only for the prints. At first, each one dug deep through the drifts of soft-blowing snow with a determined downward motion. There was little disturbance besides, which suggested the walk of a person who knew how to traverse the wilderness, and I imagined they, like myself, felt the wonder and the majesty of this place. Now though, so many uncounted steps later, those prints seemed ragged. They shuffled and even staggered in places. The trail became a chaos of upset snow, microcosm landscapes churned up by unsteady feet, and I began to worry for what might wait me at the ultimate terminus of this increasingly pandemoniac mess.

It was when the trail finally lost all cohesion and seemed at last to have been made by someone crawling rather than walking, that my own will began to falter. The fear of what I must now be rapidly gaining on, the fear that had dogged me since before I ever ventured down this cursed trail, the fear of this whole world, whose frozen, midnight, nightmare essence finally revealed itself to me. This was not our world. Our warm world, untouched by the endless grinding ice that had remained since time immemorial at the edge of sanity, was nothing to this. It was a fluctuation; it was an imposition. It was a blemish, a blemish that the ice and snow toiled annually to obliterate. I felt the anger with which the winter recedes every spring and understood why so many ancient rituals and festivals were performed and remembered as a way of ensuring the victory of the spring and the defeat of the snow.

The snow. The snow that has been the same snow since before humans crawled in the sand, before the sun climbed the sky, the snow that can be melted, kept, held in another, life giving-form, but which will always return to deathly, eternal ice in merciless mockery of the creatures it once nourished. It was these thoughts that resounded through my consciousness when my strength failed at last. And in that moment, I felt that it was good. I had stood before the Gods of the Snow, and I had fallen. This was as it should be, this was right.

That was most likely the hypothermia, or exhaustion, or my own waking dreams, or some hellish combination of all three. But those vivid impressions of that icy world, so alien to our own and so pitiless to it, seem to have been what made me give up at last and come to land, sprawling amid the scattered prints of that which had crawled there before me. And it was then that I saw the final thing that drove the last shred of sanity from me, that shattered the last solid certainty that remained to me after that nightmare march through those forsaken regions at the end of the world. It was almost amusing, here at the end, to think that those prints will soon melt away, like my words, when spring comes to wage its war on the Ice. Then nothing will be left, nothing, until the snow comes again and mockingly shows us the paths taken by those that came before us. That shows us our own path stretching out behind us, and that records for a while, the real banal happenings of that blemish, that mistake that is all life on Earth.

What I saw, when my face connected with that snow, when my floundering arms pulled my eyes free of the clogging drifts, was nothing more or less than a footprint, preserved by unhappy chance or crafty cold, in perfect frozen accuracy, a footprint. A single print which I could not, even in my state of near collapse, mistake for anything other than that of my own booted foot.

✕✕✕✕✕✕✕✕✕

About the Author

Andrew Benn is a writer living and working in Glasgow, Scotland. He studied philosophy at university, but he doesn't let his deter him. He spits his time between freelance writing and freelance gardening. He writes mostly weird fiction, suspense and horror stories, and he works mostly rural and private gardens.

EATING CHILDREN

Elana Gomel

Xiaoling climbed out of the car and walked through the no-man's land toward the brightly lit fence, her feet whipped by flying litter. Her belt-pack chirped.

She stopped in front of the fence, arms pressed to her sides.

"Name?" the fence asked.

"Dr. Cynthia Li."

"Invitation?"

"Mrs. Estella Lewis, 22 Paradise Drive."

The fence appeared to clear its brass throat.

"Reason?"

"Patient's home visit. Mrs. Lewis' son Timothy is sick."

The pack chirped again, but she knew better than to attend to it or to make any sudden movement whatsoever. Let Mrs. Lewis stew a little. It was not her fault that she was late. The road had been blocked.

"Step forward!" the fence commanded. "Hands on your head, fingers interlaced, look straight ahead."

Xiaoling obeyed, her body on auto-pilot as her mind again went through the list of Tim's symptoms as described by a sobbing Estella. The list made no sense.

A pinprick of red light as her retina was scanned. A tickling sensation in her chest, which she assumed to be psychosomatic, since portMRA was supposed to be undetectable.

"Shoes off. Put your pack aside. Turn around slowly."

Finally, it was over. She picked up her pack, wriggled her dew-damp feet back into her cloth shoes, and walked through the reluctantly retreating fence.

Harmony Gardens at 3 a.m. were as placid as they would be at 3 p.m., with the additional bonus of artfully dimmed streetlights and the soothing sound of lawn sprinklers. Against the background of sleepy greenery and dark, nestling homes, the brightly lit Lewis residence stood out like a scream.

Estella opened the door, her eyes red, the folds of her belly peeking through the mesh panels of her housedress. Even as she respectfully listened to her reproaches, Xiaoling could not stop herself from staring at those white flabby layers, incongruous on Estella's otherwise neatly sculpted body. She knew Estella had had a womb transplant for Timothy, but were these a side effect of enforced gestation or the shameful revelation of a pill-resistant gluttony?

"He was crying in the evening," Estella was saying. "I sent Gaby, but she could not calm him down, so I went in and sat with him for a while, and he was smiling but then I woke up, and he was screaming…"

Gaby was the Lewis' housekeeper and eighteen-month-old Timothy's chief caregiver. Estella did what she could, which was not much. In all her visits to the household, Xiaoling had yet to see Mr. Lewis, though she did not doubt his existence.

A shrill scream echoed through the house, and Gaby popped out of the nursery. Xiaoling rushed past her.

She was relieved to see Tim standing in his crib, forcefully banging the rail with a teddy bear. He appeared agitated, but it was better than the lethargy of high fever.

"Hello, Timmy!" she said. He hurled the teddy bear at her and screamed again.

Xiaoling stopped. Even though the bear was now lying at her feet, Tim's bare hand was beating the rail in the same rhythm but with increasing, bone-shattering strength. His scrunched-up face was mottled with dark markings as if he had smeared an entire container of baby food around his mouth.

"Turn on the light!" she commanded. She cooingly called to the toddler as she approached him. "Hello, Timmy, Timmy-boy, golden treasure…"

The ceiling poured illumination into the room, and the ugly stains on the boy's face flashed scarlet.

She caught him just as his hand, beating the relentless tattoo on the rail, gave an ominous crunch, and the screaming stopped.

She put him on the changing table and quickly examined his mouth and hands. His lips were savagely chewed, flesh hanging in tatters. The tiny fingers were peppered with bite marks. The right scaphoid bone appeared to be fractured.

Estella resumed her wailing.

"Shut up!" Xiaoling commanded. The shock of such rudeness achieved the desired result.

She pulled the diaper down and stared, aghast, at the bright pinkish-orange stain. Blood?

He had no fever. He was breathing normally.

"Do you have a new pet?" she asked. It was Gaby who answered.

"No. Only Caesar and Molly."

Caesar was a borzoi and Molly a gen-engineered hairless cat.

"Get rid of them!"

"But Dr. Singh says they're necessary for Timmy's development!" Estella protested. Dr. Singh was Tim's psychiatrist, but more to the point, the animals were Estella's constant companions.

"Nevertheless!" Xiaoling had learned to relish her rare moments of power.

"I'll kennel them for a while," Estella conceded sulkily.

The nursery had a complete medical station. Xiaoling quickly disinfected Tim's injuries, sprayed them with a liquid regenerator, and pumped him full of baby sedatives. When she was done, the toddler was peacefully asleep.

She turned to Estella, whose tearful dependency was waning in sync with Xiaoling's treatment. By the time the boy was back in his crib, the mother was yawning conspicuously and tapping her foot.

Xiaoling regarded her silently, her face devoid of any expression beyond professional attentiveness. She knew what would have happened in such a case fifty years ago. The police would have been called in on suspicion of child abuse. But nowadays, only shadow towns were mentioned in connection with child abuse.

She had to proceed very carefully. She could not afford losing her employment visa.

"Timmy is all right now," she said (*always reassure the patient first, as they taught her in ex/med school*). "But I would like you to have several of my colleagues come visit at first opportunity: an endocrinologist, a pediatric surgeon, and a child-development specialist. I'll comm you the names today."

"I heard they were lifting quarantine in one of the townships…" Estella said ominously.

"They are not. And even if they were, Tim's problem has nothing to do with proscribed towns."

Estella nodded reluctantly, but Xiaoling could see she was not convinced. At least, she managed not to say "shadow towns"; that was politically incorrect.

On her way out, Xiaoling poked her head into the staff kitchen. She had a raging thirst. At home, she would willy-nilly drink tap water, but if she could taste delivery supply, why not?

The tap bore the trademark logo NP, Naturally Pure. She poured half a glass and a smooth intoxicating coolness filled her mouth.

Before leaving, she carefully washed and disinfected the glass and put it back on the rack.

While driving home, Xiaoling realized she was ravenously hungry. To appease her pangs, she mentally went through the contents of her fridge. A half-bowl of cellophane noodles with tofu, some potatoes, an opened container of soy milk, plastic-wrapped crackers. She could have the rest of the soy milk and a couple of crackers now and bake the potatoes for dinner. She had enough. Life was good.

Absorbed in the memory of a basket of apples and pears in the Lewises' staff kitchen, Xiaoling almost hit the road barrier and fought to keep the aging Mini under control. The slick of pale light was filled with milling black figures, dipping, crouching, pushing, shoving, lifting floppy sacks, and tossing them into trucks.

State troopers were dismantling yet another encampment of shadow people who had broken out of their quarantined town on a march to nowhere. They put up no resistance, sapped by the disease, their bodies swathed in heavy protective clothes.

She watched it. Finally, the troopers pushed aside the barrier and one of them gave her a thumbs-up.

Tim died. Xiaoling heard about it from Rajiv, the pediatric surgeon she had recommended to Estella. They were far-friends, talking almost every day without ever having met. He commed in when she was puzzling over the blood tests of another patient, five-year-old Hazel.

"Fortunately, the husband has initiated divorce proceedings," he said. "She won't have the time or energy to sue."

Xiaoling nodded. The invisible Mr. Lewis must have acted quickly. She felt a distant pinprick of pity — helpless, silly Estella was on her way to a shadow town — quickly drowned by a rush of *schadenfreude.*

"They probably killed the child themselves," she said.

"Come on, Ling!" He protested. "It was a very expensive baby!"

She shrugged. Rajiv was Indian, she reminded herself, with all the residual muddle-headedness of that failed subcontinent.

"Those bite-marks," she said.

"No, it was him, the baby. I compared the casts. He already had enough teeth to do the damage."

She frowned, remembering the shredded lips.

"Why?"

"I don't know. But I'm pretty sure that when she said he had banged his head on the wall, she was not lying."

"Autistic?"

"He was social: smiled, looked you straight in the eyes. When he was not tearing himself to pieces."

Had she been mistaken? She was so sure that Tim was a victim of child abuse that she had not bothered to run a full battery of tests. The list of doctors she had commed to Estella was for her own protection, not his.

"And something else," Rajiv continued. "Elias, the endocrinologist, says the boy had a high concentration of uric acid in his blood."

"Uric acid? What does it mean?"

"I have no idea."

A high concentration of uric acid could cause gout in old people. It made no sense in a baby, though it explained the strange color of Tim's urine.

Xiaoling was about to question Rajiv some more when her mother's face floated up, overlaying his image with her anxious net of wrinkles and creases. Xiaoling quickly apologized and cut him off.

"Mama?" she said in Cantonese. "What happens?"

"Your brother is hungry," her mother said bluntly. "I feed him the spider crab's legs I found in the market, but there is no more. We only have one kilo of rice left and two buns."

"And you're wasting money on calling me?" Xiaoling yelled in frustration. "Go buy some food! What can I do?"

Her mother's lips squirmed like silent worms. Her face faded away slowly.

Xiaoling took a deep breath to calm down. She would send more food coupons tomorrow. She was almost sure they were useless. Almost.

Hazel McCarthy's face was a mask of blood. On a pink cushion under the elaborate mobile of fawns and flowers, the little girl lay as still as a ravaged doll. Fortunately for her, she was unconscious.

Xiaoling turned to face the parents. Both of them were here, Seth McCarthy, a bank CEO, and his exquisite wife. Both looked stunned.

"Who did this to her?" Xiaoling asked bluntly.

"She did it herself," Ronda McCarthy said, clearly enunciating each word. Her face, genengineered into inhuman perfection, was remote and serene. The father sighed unhappily and looked away from the dripping wound under his daughter's blond fringe.

"She has one eye gouged out," Xiaoling spat. "The other is badly scratched. Are you telling me a five-year-old took out her own eye?"

"Look, Doctor," the man started angrily, and Xiaoling realized he did not remember her name. His wife suddenly intervened.

"She yelled at me," she said with the same glassy clarity. "She yelled hateful words at me. She threw her toys at me. And then she dug into her own eyes. She is spoiled. We must return her."

Her husband slapped his wife across the face, but it had no perceptible effect. She just turned around and walked out of the room. *To call a delivery company, perhaps, to take back the defective merchandise?*

She turned her attention back to the girl, dressed the wound, injected antibacterials and pain-killers. While doing it, she paused, lifted a small hand. On all fingers but the middle one, the tiny nails were painted bright pink. The middle finger had no nail and no fingertip. It had been chewed off.

"How long has your daughter been mutilating herself?" she asked Mr. McCarthy. He had remained in the room.

"How would I know?" he barked. "I should ask you! Aren't you her physician?"

She was; and she had never noticed anything unusual about Hazel. She was as normal a little girl as she could be with a mother whose mind was whittled down to nothing by genengineering and designer drugs.

Xiaoling faced the father.

"I do not know what to say, sir," she said, realizing she was probably committing professional suicide but too rattled by the sight of the chewed-up hand and gaping eye socket to care. "Your daughter needs more help than I can provide."

He stared back at her, his bloodshot eyes revealing nothing. He was an old-fashioned kind, too proud for genengineering, keeping his own worn-out flesh. Leaving it to his wife to show off his money. Then he turned around and abruptly left the room.

Xiaoling sat with Hazel for several hours, making sure the girl was sedated, until the security team showed up and escorted her outside.

They took away her pack but she had a second one, wrapped in plastic and stowed away in a package of flatbreads. She had all her documents ready; she had consulted an ex/lawyer on how to lodge an appeal against deportation. What she did not prepare for was *not* being deported.

They drove in the windowless car for about an hour, and then she was pushed out, into the predawn chill. She looked around, disoriented. She stood in front of an electronic fence that reluctantly rolled aside as she approached, reminding her of Harmony Gardens.

But the fence was scratched and dull, its circuits silent. The air was cold and still. Finally, she realized where they had deposited her.

She wanted to run back, to scream and plead with them, to beg to be put on the first plane back to China rather than being dumped in a plague pit. But she knew it was useless. Suddenly, it came to her that this must be the standard procedure. Fuel prices were rising; they were worth more than a failed ex/med's life. The absent colleagues whose names were never mentioned for fear of bad luck had not been returned to China, India, or the Caliphate. Like her, they must have been shoved through the gates of a shadow town and forgotten.

She straightened up — dignity is the last refuge of the condemned — and walked through.

Her first sight of the shadow town was surprisingly reassuring. The houses were small and far apart, the streets clean and empty. It was a far cry from the blighted urban cores she had seen on casts. And then she realized that the impression of quietude and cleanliness came from the fact that there were no passers-by and no cars. The latter was not surprising as the quarantined were not allowed to hold a license, but she expected them to be out and about early in the morning. They could not all be dead, surely!

She walked slowly down the road. There were few trees, all of them dead. They seemed to be wearing white socks. Xiaoling blinked and then realized that the bark had been stripped off the trunks up to a man's height.

Xiaoling approached the nearest house, a dilapidated bungalow, its windows cracked, and the door hanging open. Inside, it was dim and quiet. The smell of putrefaction made her gag.

The next house was locked. She had to walk half a block until she saw a human being.

The woman hobbled through the yard, her sackcloth dress trailing in the dirt. She pushed the hood away, and Xiaoling saw a swollen, pasty face, the eyes mere slits. She glanced at Xiaoling incuriously and started rooting in the dry soil by the base of a twisted dead tree. She scratched at the ground ineffectually and then sat down to rest. She did not react when Xiaoling hailed her.

Two children, a boy and a girl, sat in the middle of the street back to back, leaning into each other. A fly was crawling on the boy's face but he made no move to shoo it away. Xiaoling stopped at a safe distance, assessing them with a physician's eye.

The CDC was evasive about the diseases the quarantined carried, but rumors proliferated. Mutated Ebola was most commonly mentioned. Xiaoling was skeptical. She herself favored the old-fashioned bubonic plague as the most likely candidate. But the children displayed no tell-tale buboes.

Tying a scarf around her nose and mouth, she approached them. They did not seem to notice her, and when she came closer, she knew why. She had seen these symptoms before, and as she automatically ticked them off in her mind ⊠ edema, swollen stomach, listlessness ⊠ she knew they were not contagious.

The girl was holding a doll. Xiaoling squatted down in front of her and gently pried the doll from the girl's unresisting fingers. At first, she thought it was one of the old-fashioned monster toys, then she realized it was a baby, its wasted face distorted into a parody of a parrot's beak. It was dead, naturally.

"Is it yours?" she asked the girl.

"My brother," she said. The boy said nothing, but when Xiaoling lifted the baby, he made a mewing sound of protest.

"We need to bury him," she said, addressing the girl. "You know that, don't you?"

She nodded reluctantly. The boy tottered after them but then got tired and sat back in the dust.

"Are your parents around?" Xiaoling asked.

"Mum is lying down. Daddy is dead."

"Did you bury him?" Xiaoling asked. The girl did not answer.

XOXOX

During the next couple of days, Xiaoling got used to the simple rhythm of the shadow town's existence. The automatic water tank would drive through the electronic gate every other day and park in what used to be a shopping mall and was now an asphalt waste surrounded by the fringe of gutted sheds. Those townspeople who could still walk gathered there with government-issued containers in cheerful colors to collect their water ration. The food-mobile was supposed to arrive every Wednesday, but the last visit, according to the townspeople's best recollection, was about a month ago. It had then delivered a pound of nutritionally-rich gruel to every man and woman (half-a-pound for a child between the ages of 3 and 14, nothing for smaller children who were their parents' responsibility). The gruel had long been gone, along with all the mice, rats, and birds. There was a rumor that a genengineered poodle had somehow found its way into the town but the lucky family that had supposedly captured him vehemently denied it. The grass, flowers, leaves, and other vegetation had also been consumed, with the predictable consequences of poisoning and death by diarrhea.

She had survived on the fringes of the great Sichuan famine in her childhood and knew what to do. She was not overly concerned for her safety: the starvation in this town proceeded so far that the people had reached the stage of almost beatific apathy. She convinced one of the women to boil her meager stock of privet leaves and then strain the mush. The resulting greenish liquid contained no nutrients but at least it was not poisonous. The woman subsequently revered Xiaoling as a healer and so did her neighbors who occasionally came to her for medical advice. Nothing could help them, of course, but it allowed her to examine them, looking for symptoms of a contagious disease. There were none.

She had hidden her pack under a loose floorboard in the house she had taken over. There were many empty houses but most of them still held their owners. This one had no corpses, so she assumed the tenants had either died when the community still had the strength to bury its members or had gone on one of the protest marches from which no marcher ever returned. Xiaoling calculated that the food would last her for about two weeks if she ate once a night. It was out of the question, of course, to eat during the day.

Her soft living as a medical server to the rich had weakened her. She had to struggle with herself not to offer half a cracker to the girl with a dead baby brother. The girl's name was Linda; she was twelve, looking about seven, and half-Chinese, with a face still pretty because hunger edema prevented tissue collapse. But the first rule of famine was survival of one's family, and Xiaoling was her own family now.

She was cured of her tender-heartedness when one night there was a knock on the door. The door was locked; they broke it down and crowded her bedroom like embarrassed scarecrows, their swollen joints creaking audibly, and their eyes cast down in shame. Most were women because women survive famine better than men. There was only one person that she instantly classified as dangerous: a short fellow lost inside his loose skin, his once-corpulent flesh having melted away. He had the same lost look as the neighbor in her village who was shunned because of the rumor that he had survived the famine by eating human flesh.

They searched the house and found half a package of crackers that she had deliberately left in the kitchen cupboard. She cried convincingly when they tore into it, cramming their mouth full of crumbs and cellophane, their loosened teeth cracking on the hard bake. Inwardly, she was gleeful in the sure knowledge of their punishment. None of them would be able to keep the food down; with some luck, the cannibal who had the lion's share might even die of intestinal blockage. But one of the women carefully put away the single cracker she got. She lingered after the rest had gone and apologized to Xiaoling, who relented and told her to soak the cracker in water and eat the resulting mush in tiny portions. The woman survived for a time and so did Xiaoling, who still had most of her food squirrelled away.

She also had her pack. She counted on it to get in touch with her ex/med network, to inform them she was in a shadow town, and to marshal their meager legal resources to try to get her out. And she had a trump card in what she had discovered here. Even with the web splintered into nation-state islands and heavily censored, certain news had the capacity of going viral. And this was explosive news indeed. Perhaps she could parlay it into freedom.

But then she found out that the web was blocked.

Xiaoling contemplated suicide. She did not do it because she could think of no way to dispose of her body.

It was Linda who helped. She stumbled upon Xiaoling fruitlessly rubbing the dead pack and cursing in Chinese. The girl led her to the concrete barrier that surrounded the town, a crumbling though still imposing behemoth, topped with razor wire and decorated with swirls of fading graffiti. There was a place where, if one stood just so, some quirk of electromagnetic fields enabled a weak but present connection. Overjoyed, Xiaoling commed Rajiv, Elias, and others. She repaid Linda by allowing her to access an interactive cartoon.

While the girl's clumsy fingers mangled the dancing bears, Xiaoling stood over her, tensely scanning the rubbish-strewn wasteland. Her eyes fell upon the wall. Among the illegible scrawls, a fresh inscription in plain black letters stood out. EATING.

She wondered whether this was a wish-fulfillment when Linda made a protesting noise. Looking over her shoulder, Xiaoling discovered that the bear animation cut off. But the connection was not entirely lost because a black chain of letters floated out from the depth of the pad. It said EATING CHILDREN.

Neither of her colleagues answered. Salvation came from entirely unforeseen source.

She was on her way to the web-chink again when she ran into a line of state troopers. Their mirror visors reflected her startled face as they marched her down the street. They were in full battle gear and asking questions of them was as futile as conversing with Humvees.

There was an armored vehicle, low-slung and lizard-green, parked outside the barrier. They pushed her in. There was a man sitting in the back.

"I asked them to treat you well," he said almost apologetically.

"How is Hazel?" she asked, smoothing her pants as she sat down beside him, their knees almost touching.

"Hazel is dead," he said.

She tried to say "I'm sorry" and could not.

"She died because she tore out her own windpipe," he continued tonelessly. "Marina…my ex-wife…she left her alone. She called for a visit-nurse, and then she walked out."

Now she could say she was sorry. Dying was one thing ⊠ she had seen too much of it in the last couple of days to be impressed. But dying alone…

"I've heard of five such cases in the last two months," he continued. "My business acquaintances. My friends. Children killing themselves. Biting off their own fingers. Tearing their mouths. Dying."

"All in gated communities?" she asked incredulously.

"Yes," he said, "all in gated communities."

Xiaoling was silent, her mind busy calculating her options.

"The government is expelling ex/meds," Mr. McCarthy continued. "But they have to tread lightly because people won't be left without their doctors."

"Are you telling me I'm being expelled?" she asked.

"No. I'm telling you I'm hiring you as my private physician and extending your visa."

"Why?"

"Because I want you to get to the bottom of this. It's an epidemic of some sort, and the CDC is bullshitting, as usual. Blaming a contagion from the shadow towns!"

"How do you know it's not?"

He stared at her with dark-ringed eyes, and she saw he had not been sleeping well recently.

He must have really loved his daughter!

"You've been here for some time now," he said contemptuously. "Should I be afraid of you infecting me?"

"No," she said, "hunger is not a communicable disease."

"Precisely," he said, and she realized that her great discovery was no discovery at all.

Nothing more needed to be said. He commed all the necessary documents, made her sign a ten-page-long disclaimer, and drove away with her in the back. What she had taken for a military vehicle was, in fact, his private car.

Full access to the web was a dizzying luxury, and she spent a couple of hours just paddling in the ocean of information only to discover that it had become a Sargasso Sea, tangled with black seaweed.

The words floated in the web in many different forms. They festooned the headlines, popped up as banners, even slithered across videos and 3Ds.

EATING CHILDREN

It was happening, she knew. In famines, some reverted to beasthood, preyed upon children and the old. Babies were killed and consumed. It had happened in the past, and now, with the global economic collapse, hunger had reasserted its dominion, and the age-old patterns of behavior had resurfaced. In shadow towns and shadow countries, people ate grass, pets, and occasionally, each other. Since the famine babies were doomed anyway, why should they not contribute to their families' survival?

So what was the point of this annoying web-virus? Appealing to the conscience of the rich? Xiaoling shrugged, shook the black strings of words off her pack, and continued her search. They had known it all along. Food prices being what they were, there was no possibility of feeding all the hungry mouths. Better to lock them up and pretend they were dying of an exotic and unconquerable disease than of the mundane and depressing malnutrition.

But there *was* an exotic and unconquerable disease, striking — astonishingly — the children of the well fed. Seth McCarthy was right: there had been five such cases in Harmony Gardens and the nearby clusters. A short search uncovered ten more. And if she were to earn her own daily bread, she had to find out what it was. Mr. McCarthy would not hesitate to dump her back in the famine-land if she failed.

She got in touch with the ex/meds who had cared for the dead children and reviewed their files. The victims had suffered from no neurological disorder, and there had been no viral or bacterial infection in their blood.

Mr. McCarthy walked in upon her one evening when she was combing the web, feeling that her fingers were wearing holes in her pad. He looked over her shoulder. She lifted her head and met his glazed eyes. It occurred to her that he wanted her to go to bed with him, which of course she would do.

But he did not seem to be interested. His face was dark as if the bruises of fatigue had permanently soaked into the skin.

"I've been laid off," he said. "Heavy losses in the last quarter."

She waited.

"I can't retain you any longer," he continued. "I'll have to sell this house and move out."

"Move where?"

"Burbs probably. Not a shadow town. Not yet."

She waited some more.

"I've recommended you to my friends," he said. "Two children, five and seven."

"Why?" she asked his retreating back. He shrugged.

"For Hazel," he said.

Her new patient, seven-year-old Kelly, was rubbing her knee. The girl doubled over into a fuzzy pink ball, her pasty forearms squeezing from the puffed sleeves like toothpaste.

"Hurts!" she mumbled. When Xiaoling touched the swollen knee, the girl swatted her hand like a fly. With almost two hundred pounds packed into the five-two body, the slap was not insubstantial.

Xiaoling sighed. Kelly was obscenely overweight and suffering from a host of related conditions, including stupidity. But she was too young to have arthritic joints. Nevertheless, the knee was definitely swollen.

Something struggled in her memory like a trapped butterfly as she cooed over Kelly.

When the girl was finally in bed, Xiaoling found a quiet corner and pulled out her pack. Rajiv was not on the web, and she had reconciled herself to the thought she would never talk to her far-friend again. He was probably grubbing through the death-streets of Kolkata right now. But Elias, the Filipino endocrinologist…She slid through layers of media, fished in lists, plunged into forums. Finally, Elias' sketchy face appeared on the pack. He was in Manila but tenuously connected through a pirate server.

She wasted no time on condolences. She asked one question. And when he answered, she cut off ruthlessly, afraid of being tainted by association with an illegal surfer. Now she knew where to go. A standard medical encyclopedia gave her the information she needed.

She sat deep in thought when a scream came from Kelly's bedroom, and she rushed in and saw the girl bite into her plump arm, tear away a piece of flesh, and cry in terror, begging to be stopped.

"Lesch-Nyhan syndrome," she said, and Seth McCarthy's drooping face on the pack folded into a puzzled frown like a piece of origami.

"What's that?"

"A rare neurological disorder. It makes people mutilate themselves. Bite off their lips, fingers, tear off their skin, put out their eyes. It also causes high concentration of uric acid in the blood and generates gout-like symptoms."

"It causes insanity?"

"No. The patients have no control over their bodies. It's not that they want to mutilate themselves; it's more like their hands and teeth rebel, become independent. It's like being permanently attached to a predator who is trying to eat you."

"So, Hazel…"

"She wasn't crazy. She was just scared."

McCarthy nodded slowly.

"Thank you, Doctor," he said ceremoniously, and she knew that, for once, he was not blanking out her name but giving her the credit that was her due. "I appreciate it very much."

"They're going to deport me," she said.

"I know. I wish there was something I could do. But I've no credit anymore. My savings…doesn't matter. I'll have to move, too."

She nodded and wondered if it'd be to the same shadow town he had rescued her from.

About to sign off, he hesitated. "Do you know how they used to talk about the body politic?" he asked.

"Yes, I know what that means."

"I wonder if this Les…Les.."

"Lesch-Nyhan."

"I wonder how contagious it really is."

And with this, the pack went gray.

She smiled crookedly. Yes, indeed.

Lesch-Nyhan was not contagious. Vanishingly rare and caused by a single mutation on the X-chromosome, it had previously affected males only.

She waited in her Mini for more than two hours, patiently, silently, sitting in the dark, her fingertips on her muted pack.

Finally, the headlights. It was a truck, a big one, noisily rumbling through the predawn hush.

She stepped out of the car, stood in the middle of the highway, bathed in the blinding light like an alien abductee. The highlights dipped, and the truck coasted to a stop. Through the green afterimages dancing in her eyes she could see the giant NP sign.

Naturally Pure.

The driver jumped out of the cabin, and if she had any doubts, they were dispelled by his behavior. He did not yell at her, did not threaten or bluster. He just came toward her as limber as a cat ⊠ a short, thin, silent man. She looked straight at him. But her composure wavered when she saw his face.

She knew him.

He stopped, squinting at her. His left hand was tucked into his pocket curling around what she assumed was the thin tube of a sound gun. He could destroy her sight and hearing with a single flicker of his finger.

"Rajiv," she said.

He sucked in air.

"Ling?"

"Yes."

"What are you doing here?"

"Waiting for the next delivery of Lesch-Nyhan."

She felt rather than saw his fingers tightening on the tube. She lifted her pack.

"If I don't cancel my message in thirty minutes, it'll be on every public site. And I'm streaming this conversation to an encrypted cache that will be forwarded to the CDC. If I'm interrupted suddenly, it'll go off at once."

His shoulders sagged.

"Can we talk?" he asked.

"That is what I'm here for."

They sat in her car. His physical presence was less impressive than his web image: he was small, slightly hunched, and smelled of some bitter herb. His sibilant accent was more pronounced. He must have used the same web-filters that she did.

"Did you cook it up yourself?"

"No. It was done some twenty years ago by the military. They abandoned it; it's useless as a weapon, too slow. But it was really easy. It's only a single DNA misspelling, you know. It was a child's play to make a delivery virus to the X-chromosome."

"But only children are affected."

"Until the age of nine, more or less. The gene is switched off in adults. But it also works on gametes."

"So the next generation..."

"Yes."

"Why?" she asked.

He smiled crookedly.

"Do you need to ask?"

"Yes."

"Well, then, you know, we...I made a companion virus. A web virus."

"Yes, I saw. But what does it mean?"

"Light it up," he nodded at her pack. "Today is the day when the full message comes up."

She brushed the gray slate with her fingertip, and it sprang to life.

The plain black letters — EATING CHILDREN — floated to the surface as they did every time she, or anybody else, turned on their pack in the last couple of weeks. But now they shrunk to the middle of the page, and other letters, bright-red, coalesced out of the web fog, surrounding them.

THE RICH ARE EATING CHILDREN OF THE POOR

And then pictures: a quick slide show taken in shadow towns and shadow countries. She thought she saw images of the Sichuan famine but she was not sure. There had been so many.

The slide show was over, the last image of a butchered child juxtaposed with a sumptuous farmer's market fading away, and a new inscription appeared.

WE DEMAND FOOD AID. WE DEMAND END TO THE BLOCKADE.

WE DEMAND DISBANDMENT OF SHADOW TOWNS.

IF OUR DEMANDS ARE NOT MET,

YOUR CHILDREN WILL PAY THE PRICE.

And more pictures: this time of Lesch-Nyhan victims, bleeding in their high-tech cribs. She thought she saw a picture of Timothy.

IF YOU EAT OUR CHILDREN, DISEASE WILL EAT YOURS

She dropped the pack into her lap.

"Do you think it'll work?" she asked, shrugging.

"No," he said. "But I had to do something."

They sat in silence for a moment. It was Rajiv who broke it: "How did you know it was water?"

"Had to be. All gated communities use purified water, and NP is the largest supplier. Food comes from many sources."

"Clever Ling. I always knew you were smarter than me."

"But," she said, "if the next generation is already affected, what's the point? They'll just abort them, make new babies."

"Some of them do love their children."

She thought of Seth McCarthy.

"Yes, some do. But Lesch-Nyhan is incurable. Unless…"

And then she saw it.

"You have an antiviral!"

"An anti-virus, more precisely. It repairs the misspelling."

"But they'll be able to come up with it themselves! If they made the original…"

"It was twenty years ago, Ling. Since then…how many of their bio-researches are ex/meds? What do you think?"

"Ninety percent?"

"Ninety-five."

"But not all will go along with this!"

"Will you?"

She swallowed. "Children are dying!"

"Yes, precisely."

Xiaoling lowered her head.

"They are deporting me," she said quietly. "If I expose the greatest bio-terrorist attack in recent history…"

"They'll let you stay."

She stretched, banishing the kinks from her lower back. And then she caressed her pack. Rajiv was watching intently as she disabled the streaming app and killed her posting.

"I want to go back to China anyway," she said. "My mother died. I have to take care of my brother."

"I've no family in India," he said.

"Famine?"

"Typhus. Disease always follows hunger."

He opened the door and stepped out. She called after him: "Rajiv!"

"What?"

"Do you have a bottle of NP water? I'm thirsty."

He turned and looked at her in amazement: "But you know…"

"It's irrelevant. Sterilization is a condition of the visa for female ex/meds."

He nodded, dove into the truck's cabin, and came out holding an armful of plastic bottles. She drunk deeply, letting the fresh, pure water run down her chin. It was delicious.

About the Author

Elana Gomel is an associate professor at the Department of English and American Studies at Tel-Aviv University. She has taught and researched at Princeton, Stanford, University of Hong Kong, and Venice International University. She is the author of six non-fiction books and numerous articles on subjects such as narrative theory, posthumanism, science fiction, Dickens, and Victorian culture. As a fiction writer, she has published more than twenty fantasy and science fiction stories in *New Horizons*, *Aoife's Kiss*, *Bewildering Stories*, *Timeless Tales*, *The Singularity*, *New Realms* and many other magazines, and in several anthologies, including *People of the Book* and *Apex Book of World Science Fiction*. Her fantasy novel, *A Tale of Three Cities,* was published by Dark Quest Books in 2013.

AUTHORS WANTED FOR

INK STAINS ANTHOLOGIES

We are looking for unique dark fiction submissions for upcoming editions of *Ink Stains Anthology* from Dark Alley Press.

Submissions are now open for pieces 3,000-20,0000 words for all works that fit under the Dark Alley Press banner, including those in the following categories:

- Dark fiction (including lit fic)
- Gothic fiction
- Supernatural/paranormal fiction
- Horror
- Steampunk
- Black Comedy
- Fantasy

Authors of acquired pieces for Ink Stains Anthology will receive a flat fee payment upon publication. For more information, check out our website.

www.inkstainsanthology.com

Miss an issue?

Grab your copies of volume 1-4 of Ink Stains today! Available in both print and digital formats.

www.ingramcontent.com/pod-product-compliance
Lightning Source LLC
Chambersburg PA
CBHW050531260626
47157CB00004B/1562